# THE GARLICFARM GRAVEYARD IS NOT THE REASON!

ABHINAND.T

# Contents


*About the Author* — v

*Prologue* — vii

1. Gabriel's House — 1

2. An Evening — 5

3. Some Creepy Findings — 8

4. Mysterious Basement — 16

5. Happened Again — 20

6. Adaptation — 29

7. Unveiled Secret — 37

8. Friends Indeed — 40

9. The Cruise: Part I — 46

10. The Cruise: Part II — 53

11. Fight Back — 62

12. The Garlic Farm — 73

13. An Epic Tale — 79

14. Professor Explains — 92

15. Will It Happen? — 100

Epilogue — 105

# About The Author

Abhinand.T

**Abhinand.T** (born November 7,1999, Kerala) a newly risen Indian novelist, known for his science-fiction trilogy of novels called **The Pillscape Trilogy** published in the year **2024**, which includes '*The Accidental Ventures of Kiran*' '*The Damaged Pickup Truckerar*' and '*The Flambopian Escapade*'. The whole trilogy discusses the hypothetical situation that if we human beings were some puppets of one massive invisible force ready to conduct one merciless mission on the entire Universe! And what if this force possessed magical powers, and had control over scientific knowledge, time, consciousness, nature etc. His other works include the Philosophical drama "*The Forgotten Sacred Essence: An offering to Humanity*" and the Horror drama "*The Garlic* *farm Graveyard is Not the Reason!"*, both published in Malayalam and English language, in the year 2025.

The second son of Mr Thulasi C and Mrs Sudha, has an elder brother Aravind T. Abhinand earned his graduate degree in Malayalam literature, and his post graduate degree in English literature, both from Kerala University. He successfully achieved the certificate of UGC NET in English literature, which is an exam conducted in India to determine the qualification for Assistant professor in Indian universities and colleges.

He is passionate about writing, which encouraged him to become a full-time writer, specialized in existential philosophy. He is against the Alienation, Escapism and Selfishness widespread across the post-modern world, a major theme of his writings.

# Prologue

Dany is scrolling through the internet about paranormal activities, and he finds an interesting story posted by 'Fg_muthu' with the title 'Based on a true story'

(Two men, Richard and Finnagen, are relaxing on a park bench, they are strangers. Richard receives a call; he begs his wife through the phone to not leave him. Not long after, receives another call from a shylock who threatens Richard. Richard looks sad and broke, Finnagen enquires about the matter)

Richard: 'I lost my wealth, my family, my job, reputation. Everything. That one cursed message!'

Finnagen: (laughs) 'Did you not send the message to ten people?'

Richard: 'F*** off'

Finnagen: 'Sorry, what was that message? if you don't mind'

Richard: 'Do you believe in Ghosts?'

Finnagen: 'Hell no! What are you, eight? No wonder you are divorced and became a beggar!'

Richard: 'This is exactly how I insulted my friend Ben, when he explained about his weird problem with a Ghost. So, the question now is; are you willing to pass the torch?'

Finnagen: 'Go away, you moron'

Richard: 'Don't walk away, are you scared? Little baby girl is scared already... Ok, that was uncanny. But, if you are willing to take the challenge, I will give you one hundred dollars'

Finnagen: 'Ok, I am in. What is it? Do I have to go to a forest? abandoned house, graveyard? Or is there a souvenir labelled as "Cursed" I must carry? (laughs)

Richard: 'Stop kidding! You don't have to leave this bench, just repeat after me...

(Richard takes his phone out, searches for some document, opens it and asks Finnagen to read it three times, aloud)

Finnagen: (laughs) "We are all going to die, will greet soon my friend, Breta-vinemokel" (repeats three times) 'Ok, now what? Give me the hundred dollars!'

Richard: 'Yes, my pleasure' (takes out his wallet, hands Finnagen a hundred-dollar bill) 'Care to take a peek behind?'

(Finnagen takes a peek behind, then stares at Richard and asks him if he has any more challenges up his sleeves)

Finnagen: 'I must ask, what happened to you? Are you playing some social media prank or something?'

Richard: 'Did you not see that?'

Finnagen: 'See what?'

Richard: 'Weird. Ok, I will tell you what happened to me. It all happened one day, while I was scrolling through random social media posts. I don't know why I clicked that link; it was a dare. The dare to prove how courageous one was, the instructions were simple, just chant the three-line stanza three times and wait. I waited for an hour, and I do remember I was attending an online job meeting at the time it happened!'

Finnagen: 'What happened?'

Richard: 'I was sitting on my office chair in front of my work desk. Behind me was my King-sized bed, where my phone was resting peacefully. Someone called me, I picked up my phone... During that turning back for the phone pick up, I saw a glimpse of a dark creature staring at me. I dared not to turn around and inspect. Once again, took a quick peek behind... Am feeling that now!'

Finnagen: 'What was that thing? gender? Smoke or body?'

Richard: 'What! I don't know, it looked decayed, except for its sharp teeth, long nails, eyes hanging on a piece of red thread. Yes, there was a smoky aura surrounding it. Could hear it grinding its sharp teeth. I can't describe it fully, am getting cold. Please take a quick peek behind'

Finnagen: 'Ok... Nothing... Nothing...'

(Finnagen keeps taking quick peeks behind, and is laughing at Richard every time)

Finnagen: 'Are you still scared to turn around?'

Richard: 'No, it's gone. I scrolled back to the cursed post, messaged him to help me, sent him a sum of ten thousand dollars, received a different mantra, "I am dumb, I piss my pants, please don't make me melt under your wrath, Gomeco-honica" And it worked for me. The best ten thousand dollars I have ever spent even though it made me miserable and alone!'

Finnagen: 'I am actually surprised that you were once not miserable and you actually had ten thousand dollars up your sleeves once!'

(Finnagen keeps laughing at Richard while taking quick peeks behind)

Finnagen: 'Whoa! What was that? I saw it!'

Richard: 'Can you describe it?'

Finnagen: 'Similar to what you have described, what is all this? You weren't joking! What is wrong with you? Will it attack?'

Richard: 'It never harmed me, and that's all I can say. Where is your confidence? Who's laughing now?'

Finnagen: 'What is the code? to erase this dull creature!'

Richard: 'Send me five thousand dollars, you can have the code. Deal or not?'

Finnagen: 'What! You said that earlier, sure I can't recollect a single word. I don't have any money with me. I am homeless, unemployed, diabetic at twenty eighth year of age, lonely, don't have a degree... Please help me, here take this hundred-dollar bill'

Richard: 'Keep it. Now repeat after me, "I am dumb, I piss my pants, please don't make me melt under your wrath, Gomeco-honica"'

(Finnagen repeats the code more than three times, but still he finds the monster when he took a quick peek behind)

Finnagen: 'Are you sure this is the right code? Am still seeing that weird thing. Check it again, will you?'

Richard: 'Calm down. Let me check, stop screaming like a baby you big lazy man!'

Finnagen: 'How can I not! That thing is right behind my ears now! Is it going to eat my ears? I can feel it's breath. Get me out of this, quick!'

The Ghost: 'Stop screaming mister adult boy, am not going to do anything to you. To get killed; one must have some qualities in him. You're freaking homeless, and don't have a single penny or a bank account. Getting killed is the best solution to all your problems, and I am not going to help you with that. Now, get your *** out of here, run until you get exhausted and fell into your beloved grave!'

# CHAPTER ONE

# Gabriel's House

[Fifty-two-year-old Gabriel's two-story house]

8 o'clock, night. Gabriel and his wife Vinya are having a guest to please. Sam, a middle-aged man, is having a serious discussion with Gabriel while Vinya is making tea.

Sam: 'What is wrong with you! You have many pending works to do, remember. At least come up with a good solid excuse, please'

Gabriel: 'Like I said, repeatedly, I am getting hunt down by a dark mystery figure. Believe me Sam, and this thing is infiltrating my whole life. How can I work without a peaceful mind? Please don't make that funny expression, I will knock your teeth down your throat, am dead serious!'

Sam: 'Calm down man, did you visit the place I told you about? Was that helpful?'

Gabriel: 'He is a fraud. Please don't make me lose more money. I don't know what to do. It is visiting me regularly, am not even safe in my office either! Please do something man'

Sam: 'Did you commit any sinful actions in your past? Picked a fight with the gypsies? Opened a seriously suspicious box of chocolates? Took a stroll around the graveyard for fun? Are you hallucinating?'

Gabriel: 'Definitely not. I was cut by it last week! And it still hurts'

Sam: 'Why don't you tell Vinya about this? she will be supportive. Stick around with her because Ghosts only attack the lonely ones'

Gabriel: 'How can I tell her? She will think of me as less manly and a coward! I don't want that to happen'

Sam: 'Well. Ok, do this. Next time it appears, directly ask it about why it is hurting you?'

Gabriel: 'I am not that courageous, but your idea is worth a shot. I will try my best'

Vinya interrupted their heated discussion with her tea tray arrival. The trio starts drinking tea, Sam is doing weird actions with his eyes that translates to asking Gabriel to tell Vinya about his weird problem, but Gabriel rolls his eyes at him.

Sam: 'Sister, what is your opinion on Ghosts? Are they real? What is your attitude towards people who believe in this kind of stuff?'

Vinya: (laughs) 'They should be put into an asylum; there is no other way. Madness needs to be treated the earliest. I once participated in a dare and won five hundred dollars. The easiest money I have ever made'

Sam: 'What was that dare?'

Vinya: 'To spend six hours inside a haunted mansion, alone!'

Sam: 'You are very brave. Gabriel, you should be proud to have a wife like this'

Gabriel: 'Yes... Am already... It is getting late, perhaps we should wind up this meeting and get some sleep'

Sam: 'That's rude, but true. Goodbye'

Sam leaves, Gabriel and Vinya wind up their day and get to bed at 9 o'clock. Gabriel looks troubled, he slowly climbs the stairway to his office room to do some of his unfinished work.

11 o'clock night, heavy rain mixed with thunderstorm keeps quaking the whole area. Gabriel is working on his laptop; alone in his office room. Looks like he is not completely dedicated to his work alone, he has something in mind. He looks confident and is waiting for the obvious to happen anytime soon. Gabriel is done with the cat and mouse play; he wants to confront his demon or whatever that was causing him uneasiness.

He is sweating a little, suddenly, something pulls him down to the ground, makes few slashes on his body, Gabriel is screaming. The invisible intruder looks like a dark shadow that constantly keeps getting bigger and smaller. An aura of death is enveloping this dark shadow. The thunderstorm roaring outside made Gabriel's screams useless. He got back to his feet, the hard pain he is experiencing from the cuts, made him strong as a pillar of sudden courage.

Gabriel: 'Who are you? What do you want? Kill me now, stop playing!'

(silence)

The dark shadow swallows Gabriel and immobilises him in an instant. He is screaming nonstop, and surprisingly the dark figure made Gabriel shrink down to the size of a cup, he is completely covered by the thing like a bedsheet dropped over him. Finally, it detached from Gabriel, he turned back into his original size. He is shivering and is terrified to the extreme. He is never going to have a chat with it again.

Gabriel manages to get back to his feet again, runs out of the office room, makes a trail of blood behind him, gets rolled down the steep staircase. His wife finally finds the injured Gabriel lying on the ground, his eyes are almost popped, lack of breath and heavy sweating made him pass out at once.

(loud scream)

6 o'clock dawn, sunny weather, birds singing in wind's rhythm. Gabriel's house is filled with vehicles, and a huge crowd. Weeping noise covers the entire place. Gabriel's funeral is going on but they are waiting for someone's arrival. The crowd is getting frustrated with the delay; they keep critiquing the missing person.

Stranger: 'What is the need of waiting for him? All he will do is mocking us for our beliefs and values. Let someone else do the rites'

Stranger: 'Yes, let someone else do this. Time is getting wasted, the dead body has started to decay. At least make a call for him!'

Stranger: 'Stop arguing, he must come and do the rites, or else Gabriel's soul would never get to heaven. Calm down, he is on his way. If any of you have a problem with this, please leave!'

# CHAPTER TWO

# An Evening

[On the top of a hilltop]

Thirty-three years old Dany and his wife Lacy are enjoying the beautiful dawn from the top of the Figsnig hilltop. They are alone here and are enjoying the peaceful nature.

Lacy: 'The legends are true! I can feel the nature fairy caressing my cheek muscles, and the rays from Sun God filling my body with peace'

Dany: (laughs) 'It's not because of Sun God nor the Fairy, but please thank to your unemployed state. Why can't you speak like normal human beings?'

Lacy: 'Come on dear, stop harassing me. I will get my dream job soon, and don't ever call me a fool'

Dany: 'Sorry, I didn't mean that way. You do know these kinds of mythological stuff makes me angry. You're the one who made me say it'

Lacy: 'Stop judging people for their beliefs. Just for once pretend like you are a believer of these mythic assumptions, am sure you will find your peace finally'

Dany: (laughs) 'Don't worry about my peace, am little frustrated only because of the global recession thing'

Lacy: 'Come, let's take a stroll around this hilltop, find something to eat, fight off wild beasts if we have to'

Dany: 'As you wish, young lady'

Dany and Lacy start wandering around the hilltop that is filled with stones and overgrown grass. They start eating random berries from suspicious looking bushes, pet different human friendly animals pasturing around the place, sure it is not a wild hilltop but some kind of artificial vacation destination. They drink water from a small pond filled with fresh leaves, and are getting busy inside the pool, embracing their primal genes. They resume their walk, both make stop after seeing a hoard of baby rabbits hiding under a stone. Lacy cracks a smile

Dany: 'Why are you laughing at them? They look cute'

Lacy: 'Oh, I wasn't laughing at them. It was this thought of your mother telling me to give her a baby to love and take care of'

Dany: (laughs) 'My mother? definitely not for love but to show people that I have no problem producing a baby, am manly and perfectly alright'

Lacy: 'Come on, don't be silly. It's your mother. And we have been married for five years now; she spoke from her heart'

Dany: 'Ok, whatever. Let's continue walking'
(silence)

Dany: 'You keep thinking about that baby thing?'

Lacy: 'Kind of. I mean, I think am ready'

Dany: 'What! I warned you not to see too many of those emotional drama things scattered all over the Television'

Lacy: 'I think it will be great, be optimistic dear. You have a good job, and your parents are getting older, they do have dreams'

Dany: 'They had dreams, not anymore. Why people don't care about their own happiness! They are just following the boring pattern repeatedly, for some kind of eternal reward for all the sadness, and then they rely on their children to provide what they never had in their life... Let's not ruin this small vacation talking about my parents' happiness, come let's get back to the tent. I must turn on the server soon'

Dany and Lacy make haste to the tent; Dany is a little frustrated with what happened with him and Lacy. He keeps accusing Lacy of killing the mood whenever they find peace. Lacy apologises. Dany is shocked to find the number of missed calls bundled in his phone. (phone rings again) Dany takes it, apologises to the caller, and gets shocked again after hearing the news of his father passed away.

# CHAPTER THREE

# Some Creepy Findings

[At Gabriel's house]

Dany and Lacy have arrived. The angry crowd stares at them, Dany's eyes are burdened with tears, he drops to his mother Vinya's shoulder for relief. Lacy joins Dany and sits beside him and starts her consoling process.

Someone: 'It is already late, come on Dany, get ready to do the funeral rites. Gabriel's body is getting worsened'

Dany: (weeping) 'Will that revive him back to life? What is the need... Leave me alone... Let me cry'

Lacy: 'Sir, give him a minute, he will come'

Lacy pleads with Dany to do the funeral rites to satisfy the crowd, but he rejects her pleas. Anyway, Vinya's strong words are enough to make Dany forget his atheist side for some time. He runs inside the house, gets changed and does the funeral rites with guidance from the priest.

Collision occurs when Dany heard someone mentioning his dead father as a madman. Dany fought the man named Febin, and his friends, police arrival made the fight stop finally. Dany and Febin are taken to the police station.

Officer: 'Who do you think you are?'

Dany: 'He called my father a madman!'

Febin: 'What's wrong with that? Your father spent a hefty amount on researching about how to get rid of ghosts!

We all have the same opinion; he is a madman'

Officer: 'Yes, we do. He once filed a complaint against a dark ghost, showed us many cuts all over his body. He even had the courage to rip off his dress (laughs) Sorry son, we called you about the matter but... you remember your response, right?'

Dany: 'I thought you were playing jokes on me because of my non-believer attitude! What happened for real? My father was assassinated?'

Febin: 'No, we also thought something like that, but Gabriel's drawing of the culprit solved our doubts'

The police officer puts a lot of work sorting through the dust filled record books, but finally he manages to find the page that contains Gabriel's petition along with the attachment of his drawing of the culprit. It says,

Name - Gabriel

Personal details - I don't care

Matter - There is this dark shadow figure, which keeps hunting me, and it is hurting me with its sharp claws. I don't know what to do, it is trying to kill me, please help me. It has yellow colour eyes, sharp teeth, dark fumes circling, twenty fingers on each hand with swordlike nails attached to each finger and the scariest part being it can resize its body profile constantly.

(Drawing of a figure that does not possess any human resemblance, but similar to the ghost image – a bedsheet tossed over a person and two circles drawn on the head part – used to draw by third graders)

The police officers and Febin are laughing hard each time they peek a look at the funny drawing. Dany is embarrassed.

Dany: 'Sir, please let me have this page, I can't handle this kind of humiliation. Here, take these five hundred dollars'

The officer immediately took the money and tore the page off from the record book, handed it to Dany. Dany folds it four times, stabs it into his pocket with sheer aggression.

Officer: 'Calm down son, you are also guilty in this case. Don't stare at me angrily, you do know we have tried to inform you about the matter. This wouldn't have happened if you had listened to our words'

Dany walks all the way back to his house; the crowd has dispersed. Vinya, Lacy, Sam and a few others remain. Vinya is still weeping; Lacy keeps telling her that it is all part of God's plan. Dany is getting frustrated again, he storms into Gabriel's office room, angrily swipes off the table, starts searching for something...

(Intense breathing) Dany feels the presence of someone standing behind him. Dany starts sweating, he slowly makes his turn around. It is a figure with a human shape.

It: 'Take it easy Dany, am not an intruder. My name is Madhav, I was working with your father, at the tax department. Just came here to retrieve some documents, have asked your mother's permission'

Dany: 'Stop hiding... Can't you wait a day?'

Madhav: 'Sorry boy, your father hasn't done any work since last year; he was after that mysterious figure, and he didn't even take a long vacation either'

Dany: 'When was it first happened? his crazy reactions?'

Madhav: 'I don't know the exact, but definitely last year. He had me go with him to a priest, and spent ten thousand dollars to conduct a ritual, but it was of no use'

Dany: 'Ten thousand! What! Are you insane! Then what? Any more spending's?'

Madhav: 'Yes, of course. Gabriel spent over a hundred thousand dollars on a variety of rituals. He even swallowed a snail, part of a ritual, and got sick for a month. Where were you all this time? Did you visit him last year?'

Dany: 'I was in Switzerland, for my job. I work at Qweruse IT company. No one had the pleasure to inform me about what has happened here, my mother only told me, "Everything is fine" What was that?'

Madhav: 'Gabriel knew what your response would be if he confessed to you, his issues. Even i am sure you would have thought less of him, right?'

Dany: 'Not a doubt! What was wrong with him? Did he see some weird horror films and was caught in that?'

Madhav: 'I don't know. Listen boy, am in a hurry, please help me find the files'

Dany and Madhav started their aggressive search. Swimming through a pile of paperwork, record books, met friendly thermites and other pesky insects that has made a colony inside the documents. Finally, Dany starts searching Gabriel's office desk; he gets stymied after opening the heavy drawer.

Madhav: 'What's wrong Dany, why look so frightened – oh my! Is it alive? What is that, Cheese?'

Dany: 'No, it is a glass container filled with freaking sand! What is all this? he was crazy indeed. This is more stupidity than I already thought, I can't believe that my father turned himself into a Moron!'

Madhav: 'Stop cussing him son, maybe he had a reason for all this strangeness'

Dany: (laugh mixed with cry) 'Oh, you think... He was a brilliant tax man... Jar full of disgust looking Centipedes twisting together... Study for medical cure? (laughs) Jars of weird looking insect eggs, sand, hair follicles, decayed bird hearts, chicken feet, fisheyes, fingernails, wisdom tooth... What on earth is this yellow colour liquid, please don't tell me it is what it looks like!'

Madhav: 'I am afraid it is what it looks like, it reeks'

Dany: 'Ewww... What! Have you found what you want?'

Madhav: 'Yes, let's get out of this horror'

Dany and Madhav stormed out of the room, and for no clear reason, they shut the door hard, locked it by wrapping a towel around the door handles. Madhav left the house immediately, and after an hour, the Gabriel house is back to its family members alone. Dany, Lacy and Vinya keep staring at the ceiling, a storm of silence compressed the whole room.

Dany: 'Mom, do you believe in Ghosts?'

Vinya: 'Ewww... Where did you get that from?'

Dany: 'Just curious. What about father, was he a believer? And most importantly, what strange incidents happened here last year. And for what you people repeated "Everything is fine" repeatedly when there was a pile of mating Centipedes forming a whole civilization inside a jar of glass?'

Lacy: 'Am sorry, was that Centipede thing a metaphor?'

Dany: 'Shut up! This is between me and my mother, answer me mother!'

Vinya: 'Stop yelling at me Dany! Have you lost your mind? I don't know what happened to Gabriel, there was only this one incident where he asked me to accompany him, to a fraud sorcerer living somewhere I can't recollect now'

Dany: 'Did you agree to it?'

Vinya: 'What! No, I mocked him so hard enough to not bring up such kind of subject ever again. Happy son?'

(Doorbell rings) Dany attends the door. It is a crowd of ten plus people, not looking friendly at all.

Dany: 'What's the matter guys? Why so angry?'

Guy: 'We need our money back! We know this is a hard time for you and your family, but we have family. Here, check this file, this contains documents signed by your father when he loaned moncy from all of us. Please settle us all before the end of this month'

Dany takes a closer look at the file, meanwhile the group of visitors have left the house premises. Dany is shocked to the point he lost control of his lower body. He dropped to his knees, grasps for air. Lacy and Vinya sensed the heavy beating of Dany's heart...

Lacy: 'What happened dear, did they attack you?'

Dany: 'Not them, but my dead father!'

Vinya: 'What!'

Dany: 'The visitors were money lenders from all around the world! Am not joking, this file contains legal notices from world banks'

Vinya: 'For what are they targeting us for? Have you made any mistakes?'

Dany: 'Don't you still get it? My father has taken loan from numerous people, and from other money lending institutions all around the world. The whole total is... Seven hundred and eighty-three thousand dollars! What the!'

Vinya: 'Oh my, that's why he went on many vacations alone. You dirty liar! How could you?'

Dany: 'What vacation? When?'

Vinya: 'Six months ago, he explained he was done with working all his life, wanted fresh air, bid farewell, travelled all around the world alone, came back after two months! How could he cheat on me!' (cries hard)

Dany: 'Calm down mother, he went on all those journeys to collect money, for some big purpose or an event. We must find it'

Vinya: 'Sam can help us; he is the manager of the bank where Gabriel has his account'

Dany: 'That's great, ask Uncle Sam to send the transaction details of father'

Vinya calls Sam for help, meanwhile Lacy and Dany go out. Dany stops the car in front of a theatre complex.

Lacy: 'Why here?'

Dany: 'What kind of a question is that? See a movie'

Lacy: 'Shouldn't we wait a few more days? people will judge us for this. Don't laugh, am serious. We are supposed to be sad for some time, aren't we?'

Dany: 'I am sad. But I am so frustrated with all the creepy ways my father has taken to pull our family into heavy debt. Do those people you say judge us help us? No! I need some time to relax my mind, the company keeps calling me, you know I can't work when am surrounded by unwanted mysteries'

Lacy: 'I know. If you want to have some peaceful time, let's go to the beach'

Dany: 'Agreed. Honestly, the new releases have pathetic reviews. Let's go to the beach then'

Dany and Lacy make way to the beach, but Dany takes a sudden stop after noticing something. He takes a quick reverse, stares at a notice, he looks bewildered.

Lacy: 'What's wrong? Who is this?'

Dany: 'Madhav! An employee who worked with my father. We met yesterday, in our house. Come on, let's take a look'

Dany and Lacy leave the car, take a narrow route, walk all the way to Madhav's house. There is one crowd standing, the funeral rites are underway. Dany enquires about Madhav's unusual death, the stranger replies that Madhav had a stroke last night. Without wasting anymore time, Dany and Lacy leave the spot. They get to the beach; Dany hasn't spoken anything since they left Madhav's house.

Lacy: 'Speak something dear, are you worried about the possibility of a supernatural force haunting us?'

Dany: (laughs) 'What? Why? And what kind of supernatural thing are you talking about?'

Lacy: 'Like a Ghost? Maybe our house is haunted. What do you think?'

Dany: 'How can you think like this after all these years living with me. Let me explain what has happened; Coincidence'

Lacy: 'Agreed. I forgot to tell you that your mother again requested me to give her a baby. What you think?'

Dany: 'From where she mustered the courage to request you! In the middle of all these horrors! you think am boring?'

Lacy: 'Where did you get that from? You're the sweetest'

Dany: 'Ok then. Its settled, we are going to wait two more years'

(phone rings)

Dany: 'Hello... Uncle Sam... Where?... Ok, I will be there in half an hour (hangs up) Lacy, its uncle Sam, he has taken the transaction details of my father. All our doubts will be cleared soon'

# CHAPTER FOUR

# Mysterious Basement

[Dany and Lacy go to see Sam, who is waiting inside a cafe]

Sam: 'Hello couple, how are you?'

Dany: 'Fine, tell me about the transactions, any international ones? I need some of their contact information'

Sam: 'Calm down son... No international transactions, but Gabriel has collected a hefty amount from various money lending institutions around the world, in the last four months! He used most of the sum on this specific person, The Devil Slayer'

Dany: 'How much did he spend on this weirdo?'

Sam: 'About four hundred thousand dollars!'

Dany is speechless, his eyes overflow with tears, face has turned red and swollen, hands are shivering, legs are unstable. Lacy holds him with all her strength.

Sam: 'Don't worry son, we must file a complaint, come with me'

Sam helps Dany and Lacy get into his car, drives to the police station. Alone, Sam runs inside the station. Lacy keeps comforting Dany, but his questions are not friendly. After a full hour, Sam is back.

Dany: 'What happened uncle? Can we find him? let's go and catch that son of a *** hurry up uncle, revv the engine'

Sam: 'Sorry son, we can't do anything about this person. He is a fraud and is a most wanted criminal. The police have been searching for him for over a decade, still couldn't find a scratch'

Lacy: 'Uncle, did they tell you something about what is this person's mode of fraud?'

Sam: 'He sells fake souvenirs that, according to him, kill Ghosts. And he also does fake rituals to counter the deadly spirits. Calm down son, your father made a mistake, forgive him'

Dany: 'Forgive him? We have received death threats for him not paying back the massive loans he took'

Sam: 'I am sorry, is there anything I can do for you?'

Dany is speechless. He keeps thinking about something. Sam and Lacy remained silent to let Dany figure out what he is thinking...

Dany and Lacy are back in their house. Without wasting a second, he confronts Vinya

Dany: 'Mother! The key to the basement, where is it? give it to me now!'

Vinya: 'How dare you yell at me! Am your mother'

Lacy: 'Cut the philosophy dear lady, this is not the right time to lecture. Where is it?'

Vinya runs back to her room, ransacks the whole room, finds the key and gives it to Dany, he slowly walks to the basement door, but struggles to find out how to open the unusual looking door lock that is in the shape of a skull wrapped around two hissing snakes.

Lacy: 'Is this your first time entering this room?'

Dany: 'No, this lock is new. Am getting a weird feeling about what we are going to find inside!'

Vinya: 'Gabriel had this secret space for himself since last year, he never let me take a peek inside this room'

Finally, after many attempts, Dany opens the lock, slowly opens the door, a strong gust filled with the aroma of herbs and essential oils rammed into the trio's nostrils. After taking some time to get adjusted, they entered the basement. Once again, Dany is frozen like a statue. The basement is stacked with unusual looking objects, a golden colour staff with a scary hand fixed on top, five human skulls original or not, a square container made of bones, a non-perfectly cut stone having some weird inscriptions, a large vessel containing strong smell powder, and finally a medium sized glass jar containing green grass and bugs. The trio runs out of the basement while screaming...

Dany with his shaking hands, somehow manages to shut the door. A wall of silence swallows the house, the trio is exhausted, take rest on the couch and ground. Next morning has arrived. Vinya wakes up Dany and Lacy; they all agreed to never discuss about the mysterious things ever again. Finally, the serious air has left the house, Dany cracks an absurd joke about the whole madness brought to the family by his dead father. Lacy and Vinya laughed with their own jokes dropped in to the mix. Dany leaves the hall, takes a bath and is ready to go somewhere.

Lacy: 'Why getting dressed? Am I not invited?'

Dany: 'Are you interested in coming to "Rejendra Software Solutions" for an interview for the post of leading software developer?'

Lacy: 'I shouldn't have asked. But what happened to your previous job?'

Dany: 'They fired me without notice; I don't know what happened. Inflation maybe'

Lacy: 'That's surprising. You were the leading engineer of that company. How could they let you go? And what about this company. Where did you find about it?'

Dany: 'Someone emailed me to please attend their interview and join their company. Almost six figures a year basic pay!'

Lacy: 'Did they really say "Please"? sounds not right'

Dany: 'I know, but we need money, or they will kill us all, remember?'

Lacy: 'Yes. Can I have three hundred dollars? I have ordered some cosmetics online'

Dany: (gasps) 'What! How dare you keep wasting my hard-earned money! Do you know the value of a single dollar? Of course not. I am walking on a metal thread all my life to put food on your table, while you are casually wasting your life away watching stupid TV programmes'

Lacy: 'Enough! I am cancelling the order'

Dany: (laughs) 'I was just joking. Sorry dear (laughs) why you always fell into my prank traps?'

Lacy: (cries) 'You think... Funny... Am loser... Am bored... I don't want to... Live'

Dany: 'Again, Sorry dear, here is my credit card, buy whatever you want. Am so sorry. You know I don't make any unwanted purchases, please spend it for me dear'

Lacy: 'Are you mocking me again?' (cries)

Dany: 'No... Am getting late now. Ok, how about this? You take your time and plan something to scare the soul out of me, anytime you want. You know how much I hate getting scared'

Lacy: (laugh) 'Ok, but I still need the credit card'

Dany: 'No, you can't take both. Select one'

Lacy: 'I will be working on my scary plan. Better watch some horror movie scenes, your least favourite genre'

Dany: 'Nop, please give me some real experience, don't you?'

Lacy: 'You bet I will'

# CHAPTER FIVE

# Happened Again

Dany takes his briefcase and leaves. An hour later, he arrives at his new company, receives a warm welcome from the employees working there. Dany looks bewildered because he came to attend the interview, and does that require this much attention! Also, Dany looks shocked to see the vast infrastructure of this company, sure he thought it was a start-up company. Dany meets the manager.

Manager: 'Welcome to our family, Dany. My name is Auber, the manager of this global company'

Dany: 'Thank you sir, when will be my interview?'

Manager: 'There is no interview for you... Here is your identity card, your office is on the second floor. Have fun'

Dany: 'Ok sir. Thank you for this opportunity'

Manager: 'Why thank us? We thank you' (laughs alone)

Dany makes way to his work cabin. It is heavily decorated and fully air conditioned enough to have a perfect sleep on the soft cushion bed; pride-fully resting in the corner. He is not sure what to do, but then he finds an envelope containing a paper filled with all his work objectives. Dany starts working, but after an hour, transfers himself to the bed, calls Lacy to describe his new paradise.

Lacy: (silence followed by a sudden boom sound) 'Did I get you? Are you irritated right now?'

Dany: 'What are you, five? Even kids won't get scared from that' (laughs)

Lacy: 'Come on! It is not the worse, is it?'

Dany: 'Cut this out, is mother doing okay? I feel guilty for yelling at her yesterday. Is she inside?'

Lacy: 'Yes, she is sweeping the house'

(silence)

Dany: 'Oh no! Lacy, you must stop her from entering father's office room. Hurry, no questions, just go!'

Lacy gets terrified; she rushes to Gabriel's room. Dany's assumption was right, Vinya is using Gabriel's personal computer planted inside the office room, she is reading something on it'

Lacy: (heavy breathing) 'Mother... We should... Leave this... Here speak...'

Lacy gives the phone to Vinya, meanwhile Lacy struggles hard to get back to her normal breath pattern.

Dany: 'Mother please get out of that room immediately, I will explain why later'

Vinya: 'Son, what is the issue? Explain. Are you changed into a believer of spirituality?'

Dany: 'Definitely not. There is one glass jar containing snake inside the drawer, and I believe it escaped last time somehow, be careful with that' (ends the call)

Vinya: 'He hang up. Why is he trying to get me off this room? Anyway, Lacy you don't have to worry, go downstairs'

Lacy: 'What are you doing with the computer? Need help?'

Vinya: 'Oh, it's nothing, I am just looking for Gabriel's browsing history, to really find out what he had in his mind'

Lacy: 'I know how to find it, let me help'

Vinya: 'No, please leave! Sorry darling, I don't like others reading my dead husband's internet history. You know the extreme complex mind a man possesses, right?'

Lacy: 'Ok, call me if you need any help'

(phone call)

Dany: 'BOOM! Ha ha, got you'

Lacy: 'What is wrong with you! My ears. It's not funny at all'

Dany: 'Ok, I won't do that ever again. What happened there? Did she leave the room?'

Lacy: 'Yes, she is very scared right now. So, how is your new job, exciting?'

Dany: (yawns) 'Sorry, am sleeping now. Best job ever. More payment, less work. Dream come true'

Lacy: 'I feel something wrong, is that company part of some freakish experiment base? luring human beings in and forcing them to play dangerous games, things like that'

Dany: 'How could you imagine all that stuff! you should try storytelling and creative writing'

Lacy: 'Nah, I know this story from a movie I saw last month. Take care, come home as soon as possible'

Dany: 'Don't be worried dear. Here is nothing to worry about. The thing is that there is less work to do here, and I could finish the projects scheduled for this entire month in today itself, but am not a moron to do that'

Lacy: 'Why not? If you finish it today, you can take a whole month vacation. Am I right?'

Dany: 'Wrong. If I finish all my works today, they will drop a new pile of work on top of me, there is no escape. And then I shall be forced to work in such pace for the rest of my time inside this company. I would rather die than that!'

Lacy: 'Ok, have fun with your work time sleep, bye'

Dany ends the call, continues his sleeping job. After a few minutes, the manager walks into Dany's cabin without any notice, wakes up Dany.

Dany: 'Sorry sir, I am having a bad day, headache and...'

Manager: 'It's okay Dany. How's the office? Everything good?'

Dany: 'Perfection. Can I have my salary on advance this month?'

Manager: 'You don't need to beg, my son. We are planning to offer your annual salary in advance to you. Happy?'

Dany: 'Umm... Sorry, what is all this about? Am sure you can find an employee for hundred dollars a year to do this job! Why me? Is this some kind of workplace agenda?'

Manager: 'What is a workplace agenda? What's cooking in your brilliant mind this time?'

Dany: 'I was thinking that maybe you don't want me working for your rival companies, thus hired me and gave child's play role here. Anyway, thanks for the money'

Manager: 'You are not hired to work this way. We have received a massive contract, and we want you to lead it. It's difficult than you think'

(message notification sound)

Dany: 'What! Two hundred thousand! Thank you, thank you very much. Oh, my goodness. Am I dreaming? Please pinch me... Aah its real'

Manager: 'Your main project will start from next month, and you must keep every information about this project confidential. Enjoy the rest of this month sleeping'

Dany: 'Sorry. What is this massive project? Little head start is good. And do I need to come here every day to sleep?'

Manager: 'Excellent question. No, you can work from home. Don't bother coming here. Bye'

Dany: 'Wait... The project. What is it about?'

Manager: 'It is just a silly one. You must create an advanced intelligence program capable of doing voice activated system developments. Clear?'

Dany: 'First, why did you say, "you must?" what about my team?'

Manager: 'There is no team, technically Yes but all of your team members including you shall be anonymous'

Dany: 'Ooh. This is going to be spicy. I have a feeling that this mission would be a threat to many IT employees working all around the world. And I believe you do know that building such a complex system sure will be a hundred times more expensive than paying the silly employees. Right?'

Manager: 'Yes, I know that. But I am just following orders. I guess the rich people want to put money into something!'

Dany: 'Poor rich people! They are so overwhelmed with all that money. Am not feeling right about this, the work ethics. And looks like heavy amount of work. You know, am in the middle of a haunting mystery thing, not good'

Manager: 'Are you seriously thinking about quitting this huge offer of money you have received?'

Dany: 'Money! I want more! Where to sign? the paper, spit it out!'

The manager gives him a pile of papers, Dany signed all of them in a rush, went back to sleep. After few hours, Dany receives another call from Lacy.

Dany: 'What's the matter now, dear? You keep disturbing my good day sleep'

Lacy: (intense breathing) 'Please hurry home... quick!'

Dany: 'Hello... Hello...'

Dany rushes out of his new office, takes his car and speeds through the traffic, gets cursed by multiple drivers, some pedestrians threw bricks at his car. Dany didn't lose his focus; reached home within ten minutes. Lacy is standing outside, carefully listening to the rumble happening inside the house.

Dany: 'What happened? Are you alright? Why is your neck red and swollen?'

Lacy: 'Your mother... She grabbed my... throat and... tried to stran... strangle me'

Dany: 'What! Is she inside the house? Come let's go to the hospital'

Dany carries Lacy into his car and drives to the nearest hospital. Lacy keeps telling him to check on his mother, but he doesn't care. Lacy is taken into the ICU unit. Dany makes way to his house to check on his mother. Though he requests help from his lovely neighbours, they rejected his invitation. The whole Gabriel house has earned the title of 'Haunted' recently. Dany went inside; he is relieved to see the basement door still locked tight. Dany loses his balance after finding Vinya feasting on the overgrown centipedes kept in jars inside of Gabriel's work drawer. Vinya is looking at something invisible standing in front of her while eating the disgusting things.

Vinya senses Dany's presence, she charges at Dany, and due to him not believing in supernatural elements; he made his stand and bear hugged Vinya tightly. She is outrageous, but Dany realised that she is not trying to attack him but trying to defend herself from someone. Dany couldn't hold her for good; she broke the hold, ran bewildered, and charged straight into the bar-less windows, crashed down to the ground covered in concrete bricks. Dany is unable to walk, somehow crept his way to the ground and fell to the ground unconscious. Dany's beloved neighbours and the police officers have filled the entire house premises. Sam took Dany to the hospital to see Lacy.

Lacy: 'What happened there? Is mother ok?'

Sam: 'She is no more'

Lacy: (cries) 'Dany, please talk to me'

Dany: (weeps hard) 'My parents... What is... What'

Sam: 'Calm down son, please don't cry'

(Weeping noises filled the room)

Sam left. Dany and Lacy stayed at the hospital for the day, crying. Relatives of both have arrived at the hospital to console them. One police officer came next day; he made everyone leave the room except the couple.

Officer: 'Dany, what happened yesterday? We have received camera footage of you staring through the broken window'

Lacy: 'What are you trying to prove here mister!'

Officer: 'Good thinking skills. Please surrender you two, or would you like to have a visit to the police station?'

Dany: (cries) 'Sir please... We... I... Leave!' (Dany screams)

Uncle Sam storms inside the room, deflects the officer's strong words. Sam hugs Dany to his heart.

Officer: 'Hey mister, get out! Else we will charge you for obstructing our duties'

Sam: 'Your duty is to find the real culprits, not to scare innocent people into it'

Officer: 'We have been spying on these two since Gabriel's unusual death, and we haven't found any other person to transfer our eyes to'

Sam: 'Gabriel's mental health was not good at that time, he lost his conscience, same with Vinya'

Officer: 'Nice trick mister, did you plan this whole thing with these two? And for your information, I have checked the medical reports, it clearly states Gabriel and Vinya lost their sense after they witnessed something terrifying'

Sam: 'The rumours are true. Gabriel's house is indeed haunted'

Officer: (laughs) 'Tell that to some eight-year-old school kid. And shut up!'

(silence)

Officer: 'Look Dany, things like these happen a lot, you people are not the first. Just surrender and accept your fate. There is nothing you can do, the case has been filed with you two as the prime culprits'

Sam: 'Sir, please. I am begging you to investigate this rather than making weird assumptions'

Officer: 'Denied! Dany and Lacy, you two are officially under arrest, and must come to the station tomorrow'

Sam: 'And then what?'

Officer: 'They will be sent to jail. Till the court makes it final verdict, they shall remain there. Find a good lawyer, hope for the best. Goodbye for now, be ready tomorrow. Don't try to mess with us, understand!'

Lacy: 'On what grounds? Are you insane? We are burned with flaming tears, and you just came to fuel its intensity'

Officer: 'Look dear, am just doing my duty. Don't hate me, the primary evidence is against you two. And the only chance you two have is to prove the existence of ghosts' (laughs hard)

Dany: 'What primary evidence! What are you trying to prove?'

Officer: 'Look son, we have been under constant pressure since your father died. He was a reputed officer at the income tax department. Gabriel died from brain damage; he was pushed down the stairway. According to our first investigation report book, it was your dead mother who pushed him. And now this murder; Dany must have found out about the role of his mother in Gabriel's death, attacked her and pushed her out of the glass window for revenge and the whole wealth'

Dany: 'How could you create false stories this easily! Look sir, I am not a believer of the ghost stuff, but we are innocent. Please investigate this further. We are not well'

Officer: 'It takes time to investigate the truth, but we can't let loose two high criminals, be ready when I get here tomorrow'

Officer storms out of the room. Dany and Lacy are not worried about by their crazy fate.

(silence)

Next morning, Dany and Lacy are ready to go with the officer. As expected, the same officer came and handcuffed them, escorted them out, forced them into the station vehicle covered by media channels.

# CHAPTER SIX

# Adaptation

Dany and Lacy are taken into the prison; they are given prison uniforms and are pushed into a disgust looking prison cell. The jailer orders them to clean the cell themselves because it is full of filth enough to call it uninhabitable, and the entire scene gives the impression that the load of waste was purposefully dropped inside the cell to punish Dany and Lacy, as a welcome treat. Dany and Lacy struggled to adapt with their new house. They are confused about the incidents that have happened in the last month.

Lacy: 'What is happening to our family? am scared'

Dany: 'It is all because of my father, he might have joined forces with some weird supernatural thing!'

Lacy: 'Since when did you start believing in this invisible stuff? What happened to your atheist veins?'

Dany: 'No. I don't believe in that, what I meant was that my parents have fallen victims to the hallucinating effects from the belief of these unreal things. I feel pity for them'

Lacy: 'How old is our house? inherited from ancestors?'

Dany: 'Please don't dig into that!'

(knock knock)

Prisoner: 'Hey you two, go to the kitchen and do your work'

Dany: 'Please leave us alone. We are not culprits'

Prisoner: 'I don't care. Don't make me come inside'

Dany and the prisoner engaged in a war of words, ended up in a fight because of the not-locked prison cell. The prison officials came at the last moment, took them away. Dany receives fifty lashes on his back, and he is sent to solitary confinement for two days. Dany is taken back to his normal cell after two days, and there he meets a new prisoner along with his wife Lacy.

Lacy: 'Are you alright dear?'

Dany: 'Yes, who is this man?'

Prisoner: 'Hi, my name is Erik, been here for nineteen years. Glad to meet you Dany'

Dany: 'You sick pervert, get out of this cell. I am her husband. Did he attack you?'

Lacy: 'No dear, just calm down. Erik is well versed in Ghost knowledge, things like that. He is willing to help us'

Dany: 'You are embarrassing yourself Lacy, have some brains! He is trying to take advantage of you. Did he perform any weird rituals on you while making you close your eyes?'

Lacy: 'Dany stop! Don't treat me like a child! I am not a fool'

Dany: 'Sorry dear, what is it you want to tell?'

Lacy: 'Erik thinks there is something wrong with our house. We should leave it as soon as possible'

Dany: 'And we did. Here we are, what's now?'

Erik: 'Stop kidding. When you two get back home, abandon all things you own including your clothes inside the house, buy a pound of animal meat and throw it inside your house, and then leave the area'

Dany: 'Man, please leave our cell. Am exhausted from all the beatings. Let me have some rest!'

Erik left the cell. Lacy starts massaging Dany's swollen back filled with lash marks. Erik brought them food for the night and left immediately. Dany and Lacy ate the food, slept in silence. Next morning, Dany goes out to do his morning rituals, but he is stopped by one prisoner.

Prisoner: 'Are you Dany? I know you are. Come with me, I need your help'

Dany: 'I have to go to the bathroom, ask someone else'

Prisoner: 'Please come, it is urgent, only take a few minutes. No one will listen to me, come'

Dany starts following him. The prisoner enters the kitchen, which is empty, orders Dany to stir the giant vessel containing some type of curry. Dany keeps stirring it with all his force, and he keeps sweating hard. Dany calls for the prisoner, but he is busy with another vessel. Dany breathes intensely, out of nowhere, a group of prisoners enter the kitchen. Dany is busy with his stirring exercise, meanwhile one of the prisoners sneak up behind Dany and covers his face with chilli powder. Dany screams aloud, tries defending with the heavy ladle. But four men grabbed Dany, made him unable to move, meanwhile one man spears a giant pumpkin into Dany's head.

Dany screams out loud, he draws a sudden spark of power, breaks loose from his captors, but can't push off the pumpkin stuck on his head. Dany runs bewildered; not taking a pause because his captors are running for him. But in reality; they are standing still and watching Dany struggle his way around hot vessels. Finally, he loses balance and falls headfirst into a pot of boiling water. He did feel the burn though his pumpkin helmet was enough to protect him fully. Anyway, the helmet has loosened, Dany shakes it off, starts swiping his eyes vigorously to get rid of the chilli powder.

The prisoners get armed with different vegetables. Dany has finally managed to make his eyes work again. Dany is enraged; he takes a watermelon to defend himself but gets beaten down by the prisoners. Dany is covered in vegetable flesh and juice, he gets caught again by four men, they force him into a barrel of flour, rolls him all around the kitchen ground. Takes him out, swings him above the boiling oil, Dany screams aggressively, blood starts dripping out of his mouth. Finally, the prisoners put Dany down and let him escape. Dany slowly walks to the bathing area; he is covered in flour mixed with vegetable pulp. Prisoners are laughing at him. Dany cleans himself and returns to his cell, joins Lacy.

Lacy: 'Your skin looks brighter, what happened?'

Dany: 'Nothing, tried a new face mask with flour and veggies'

Lacy: 'Looking good'

(Awkward silence)

Erik: 'Hey Dany, can you please come with me?'

Dany: 'Go away man, didn't you see what I have gone through to get this glowing skin!'

Erik enters the cell.

Erik: 'it was part of the prison routine. Sorry, I should have warned you, but you had no faith in me. Anyway, I have arranged bail for you two'

Lacy: 'What! How did you do that? You are kidding, right?'

Erik: 'No, here is the bail letter. You two are now officially free, please come out'

Dany jumps up, grabs the letter and reads it aggressively.

Dany: 'What the hell wrong with you! You are here for almost twenty years, who are you?'

Erik: 'I was a gypsy master, decided to move in here because science made us cease to exist. And I am damn sure you do know that you are one of them, the science one. Anyway, I have to find food, what else of an option I had then When Prison takes care of you like a baby'

Lacy: 'So, you just came here and they took you in?'

Erik: 'No, I came here, and punched the senior officer hard'

Dany: 'Good flashback. Thank you for letting us out. How did you get this? Are you part of some secret organisation?'

Erik: 'No, I know a lot of people, and you two are not officially prisoners. It is the court's decision to punish you or not'

Lacy: 'I wonder why our relatives have no interest in letting us out'

Dany: 'They do believe I killed my parents! That's why'

Erik: 'Dany, before you go, I want a small favour. Just come with me and I will show you'

Erik escorts Dany and Lacy to a secluded spot, far away from the prison habitat. Erik slowly points his finger at a specific ground spot covered in concrete, over one kilometre in radius, protected with barbed wire fence

Erik: 'Dany, see that spot, it was once a huge ditch that was used to bury the dead and the alive. If you try to stick a shovel down that concrete ground, blood will ooze out of it'

Dany: 'Is that all? Can we go now?'

Erik: 'Dany, you pride over your atheist side, and I want you to step on that concrete ground. Am sure that will change your whole perception about the truth'

Dany: 'What nonsense are you talking? Sure, I will do that for you Erik, just because you helped us get the bail.

But how do I get in? Wire wire barbed wire everywire!'

Erik: 'Oh, don't worry about that. See that unusual looking wire spot, that is a gate, always unlocked. Please be my guest'

Dany carelessly walks up to the gate; slams it open, runs inside, stops at the centre. Erik tells Dany to touch the ground, listen to the voices. Dany drops to the ground, presses his left ear on the concrete. Dany's mocking face takes a sudden hit! He keeps listening to the whatever noise he is taking from the depths of the concrete ground. After a few minutes, Erik realises that Dany has fainted, he storms inside the spot and carries Dany out. Dany and Lacy are safely escorted out of the prison; Dany is admitted in the hospital nearby. Lacy keeps shaking him, but he is still not responding. Doctor arrives to check on him.

Lacy: 'What happened? Doctor, please explain!'

Doctor: 'I don't know, is he crazy or something? Who is this dude? Who are you?'

Lacy: 'What are you saying? He is my husband; he fainted when he entered a burial ground'

Doctor: 'Crazy it is. Anyway, we need to run some tests on him to find the exact cause. And you must pay the full amount for the upcoming surgery'

Lacy: 'There will be a surgery?'

Doctor: 'No, Surgeries. Dany is in a critical condition called Cokaroko-neiumsis. His vital organs are affected, blood vessels popped all around, tissue damage, spinal cord distorted. Pay the bill and pray, may God bless him'

Lacy: 'You haven't taken any test so far, how can you tell all this? He is just scared, that's it'

Doctor gives his stethoscope to Lacy and offers a sarcastic bow of honour.

Doctor: 'Take it from here. Treat him, don't disturb us. We have studied ten years not to play video games'

Lacy: 'Doctor, please don't be angry with me. Am just being helpless here. Please save him sir, I will pay the bill in a minute'

(heavy coughing sound) Dany wakes up!

Lacy: 'Dany, don't worry dear, you just had a bad dream'

Dany: 'Hospital? What happened to you?'

Doctor: 'Don't worry Dany, we will treat her good. You are perfect now. Young lady, get to the lab'

Lacy: 'What! I have no problem. Dany, get up, let's go home'

Doctor: 'Pay the bill first before you go'

Dany and Lacy kept waiting for the bill, a well-dressed man arrived after an hour, he is holding a trophy stand with an A4 paper on top of that golden stand. The paper thing is not paper, but wood coated in shiny wax. Good amount of calligraphy is engraved into that fancy wooden bill. Dany and Lacy are shocked, not by the aesthetic appeal but the numbers written on the column labelled as 'Total' Five thousand dollars! Dany and Lacy storms into the doctor's office.

Dany: 'What is this bill? This is cheating. Our insurance is out of date, stop doing this to us'

Lacy: 'You people didn't give him any treatment except looking in his eyes. We will call the police'

Doctor: 'We did a good number of tests on him, injected several vials of medicine. Look at the back of the wood'

Lacy: 'All fake! Stop messing with us, let us go!'

Doctor: 'Oh, I see what's happening here. Lacy, young lady. When Dany and you came here, Dany was in a violent condition, and he even tried to strangle you to death. This incident made you pass out and have missed our treatment on Dany. See?'

Dany: 'Is that true? Don't you remember?'

Lacy: 'I don't know. I came, nap... scream... I don't know Dany. I can't even recollect a single event since we returned from our four-month vacation. Sorry'

Dany: 'Why are we alone? Where is... Other people?'

Lacy: 'I don't know that either, I believe I called Uncle Sam, and some of our relatives, not sure... What is happening to us dear?'

Doctor: 'Don't worry dear, you have been diagnosed with the condition called Avsadgfool-eemotisis. We have treatments available here'

Lacy: 'Fine. Whatever. Push me into it'

Lacy is taken to the surgical ward. The Doctor did unwanted treatments to her. They are finally discharged after two days. The overall bill has reached over fifteen thousand dollars. They are sure not to get back to their "happy" home, instead stay in a hotel room. The days of exhaustion and not eaten for three days, finally scraped away with a bucket of fried chicken rice and a day long sleep.

# CHAPTER SEVEN

# Unveiled Secret

Dany and Lacy wake up the next day, both have agreed not to talk for a few hours, and they announced this new agreement using hand signals. After three hours of silently contemplating on the incidents happened in the last few days, they finally end the pact.

Lacy: 'He fooled us, dang it!'

Dany: 'That Doctor? I know, how happy we were, what happened Lacy? Will we ever again going to experience happiness like we did? I don't think so'

Lacy: 'I wish I could give you one optimistic answer. Sorry dear'

Dany: 'What! Are you for real? Just throw some good feeling words at me, please. Am so hurt'

Lacy: 'I want to know what you heard from inside that concrete burial ground. Tell me!'

Dany: 'Calm down... I am embarrassed to talk about that subject; guess am not an atheist anymore'

Lacy: (gasps) 'What happened! Did you?'

Dany: 'Yes, I did. I heard voices coming out of the concrete, and am damn sure it was not coming from some fancy speakers hidden under the concrete'

Lacy: 'How do you know? They might have tricked you'

Dany: 'No! I have something to tell you that I haven't told anyone. Don't be excited, it is not a good one... After the funeral rites, I conducted a deep search on all the things my father owned. During that search, I saw something!'

Lacy: 'But wasn't that, Madhav? I do remember you talking about him ransacking the room'

Dany: 'No, this is a different incident, this happened not in the office room but... Our room!'

Lacy: 'What! Erik was right. What was that?'

Dany: 'It was an evening, I was climbing down the stairs after completing a hard search inside the guest room, where my father hid some kind of fancy bottled water. I casually entered the dining room, had some water, and was able to see what was happening inside our room, due to the opened door and the dim evening sun rays, fully capable of making the room slightly visible. And... And... I saw a dark figure looking out through the window blinds'

Lacy: 'Am getting chills, please don't tell me it was me'

Dany: 'Stop Joking Woman! It was not you, it was very big, thrice the profile you have... I was stunned. Didn't have the courage to storm inside and check...' (intense breathing)

Lacy: 'And you just stood and observed it?'

Dany: 'Yes, I was scared to move a muscle. It kept looking out, and then mother broke my stare. And it was gone forever'

Lacy: 'Maybe it was me, the lights do make my profile bigger, right?'

Dany: 'No, after a few minutes standing there, I went inside the room, but it was completely empty'

Lacy: 'We are selling the house, aren't we?'

Dany: 'Yes. I feel bad for calling my father a coward. My father was embarrassed to tell me about his ghost related issues!'

Lacy: 'But, it was true, right? I mean, you once joined the rebel group, and contributed to the destruction of a temple, just because you and your fellow rebel group wanted to spread the Atheist vibe'

Dany: 'Come on dear, why are you keep doing this? You really believe that speaking truth can console me!'

Lacy: 'Everyone has the right to hold on to their beliefs, it is not good to prey on someone who doesn't abide to your ways and beliefs, and trying to infuse your own beliefs into someone'

Lacy remained silent for a while to let Dany's anger get away.

Lacy: 'You didn't tell me about the voices you heard from the concrete burial ground'

Dany: 'I don't want to. Please don't ask me about it, let it stay with me alone'

Lacy: 'Ok. Fine. Where should we live? Can't stay in this hotel for the rest!'

Dany: 'I have received a large amount of money from the company. Let's buy a new house with it, and try to find our lost happiness'

# CHAPTER EIGHT

# Friends Indeed

One whole week has passed. Dany and Lacy are not fully recovered from the past incidents. But with the help of Dany's new friends from work, he bought a new two-story house. And he has decided to arrange a housewarming function next week. Dany is surprised to see how much friendly his newly found friends are, even though they barely know him, and the only connection they have is job related. Dany, for the first time, starts a friendly talk with his five job friends (JF)

Dany: 'Thank you guys, please stay here for a while'

JF: 'We will, don't worry about that my man. We are so sorry for the pain you two have gone through. We didn't know about all that'

Lacy: 'You people are great, where are you all from?'

JF: 'We are all from the same place called Thudorow island, heard of it?'

Dany: 'No, is it really an island or just for name's sake?'

Job friends laugh hard. One of them shows a drone shot of the Thudorow island. Dany is shocked.

Dany: 'Beautiful, I have never seen anything like this before, there is one portion of the land extended. What's that for?'

JF: 'Oh, that. It is a bridge built for fishing. The water surrounding the island has a long history of mercilessly drowning ships and boats'

Dany: 'Interesting... What about the haunted house? Has it attracted any buyers?'

JF: 'Only one person, and he is asking for a mocking number. Only one fourth the value'

Dany: 'Just sell it. Don't make any bargains'

JF: 'Don't be stuck in all the weird hallucinations you have gone through. We have planned to go on a vacation for two weeks, and we want you two in it. Please come with us, it will help you guys get better'

Dany: 'Thank you guys, we will definitely come'

Dany's job friends take leave from the house. Lacy and Dany, after a long time, spend some quality time together. But their peace gets interrupted by the loud irritating sound of police vehicle sirens. The same officer who threatened the couple at the hospital, charges into the house, making a thunderous sound by kicking open the front door. He stares at Dany and mercilessly handcuffs him and Lacy, drags them out, forces them into the vehicle and drives away. Sometime later, Dany can talk again.

Dany: 'Where are you taking us to? you cruel man!'

Officer: 'To the movie theatre, a new science fiction film has released. And sure, popcorns on me'

Lacy: 'That was very scary acting Sir, now I feel relieved... Who is starring in it, Sir?'

Officer: 'Shut up you idiots! We are going to the Court, today is the hearing. Happy prison lives ahead for both of you'

They have reached the Court, and once again the cruel officer dragged them off, pushed them into the courtroom. Surprisingly, the whole courtroom is against Dany and

Lacy, which made the officer a hero. The Gabriel – Vinya murder case is the first case of the day. The judge has arrived shortly, made his seat, gives signal to start the case trial. Dany and Lacy are placed inside the guilty square, and while taking the court pledge, the spectators spelled out their rage by booing them, but the furious judge fined them for a thousand dollars each for disrespecting the court. The serious mood demanded by the court has finally returned.

The trial is underway, public prosecutor, friend of Uncle Sam, appeared to defend Dany and Lacy. But before the trial could get into some serious debates, the judge received an envelope. He ripped it open and read carefully while the opposite prosecution rained down hideous comments and accusations over the couple and the whole modern generation, which is devoid of any empathy towards their ancestors and their parents. Judge made the whole courtroom silent with a quick strike on the desk with the wooden mallet. Judge is looking furious; he raised his voice at the officer and the opposite prosecution for fabricating the law and order.

The cruel officer felt his pride melting away, and it made him critique the judge for being biased and calls the judge a bribe baby. However, the Judge patiently explained about the report stating there is no form of evidence to conclude that someone pushed Vinya out of the window, and there are fingernail wounds on Vinya's body, and it has nothing to do with Dany and Lacy. The judge then ordered a year of suspension for the officer for disrespecting the Judge. Dany and Lacy are freed from the accusations, but Dany is terrified of the fingernail markings found on Vinya's body. Luckily, Dany's new Job friends came to the court and took them back to their house.

Lacy: 'Your new friends are amazing; I hope this vacation will help us get back to our old lives'

Dany: 'I am a monster! How can I do that to them?'

Lacy: 'Why the dramatic pause? just explain what you meant!'

Dany: 'My new job friends, they will be in serious jeopardy... Because I am currently agreed to create a program that could make them lose their job. I don't know why I accepted it, but I can't undo the contract because we have already spent most of the contract money already!'

Lacy: 'Oh, that is terrible! Do they know about this?'

(Awkward silence)

Dany: 'I don't know, but what if they know? they are trying to bond with us to secretly eliminate me! This vacation is going to be a trap. Do you really believe that some strangers will freely offer us a vacation package that costs hundreds of dollars?'

Lacy: 'Absolutely not! They are planning against us; I have smelled something suspicious about them from the start. They are mimicking the utopian ideology, I mean, that thing does not exist, right?'

Dany: 'Yes. What should I do? Only a day left for the trip, should I call and cancel?'

Lacy: 'No, that will make things more dangerous. They can make another plot; we must not let them know that you know they know about your mission. And while we are on the trip, you must convince them about your innocence by lying that you don't know how to make the machine program whatever, and tell them you are only inside it for the money'

Dany: 'That's a great plan'

(ding dong)

Sam has come to visit Dany and Lacy. They welcomed him in; Sam's face has some bad news written all over.

Dany: 'What's the matter, uncle?'

Sam: 'The news of the fingernail marks found on Vinya's body has created a pervert gossip in town. What was that Dany? Any thoughts on that?'

Dany: 'Stop! I don't want to discuss more about that subject. Please leave if you have nothing else to ask!'

Sam: 'Sorry son, I didn't want to upset you, but you were there when Vinya made that jump. Did you spot something unusual? paranormal? Maybe we should file an investigation on the matter'

Dany: 'No, I don't want to dig up my mother again! Let her rest in peace. I don't want to say this, but that house is haunted! Yes, don't be shocked. I am a teetotaller, and was an atheist, believe me or not, your choice'

Sam: 'Look son, I know you broke away from your atheist beliefs, but that is not a reason to sell away your house for some pennies! It stays in the heart of the city and still competes with the contemporary style buildings. What is wrong with you? You do know how much debt you have, and this is the solution you have to offer?'

Lacy: 'Don't blame him alone uncle. We made that decision. It is the best decision, we can't hide the truth, can we?'

Sam: 'Look dear, I am a believer of God from the moment I was born. And I have also experienced "Paranormal" moments, but I know that it was all because of my pesky brain, the creepy horror movies and stories sure made an impact on everyone's brain, no doubt... Dany, please cancel the agreement, and come with me to the police station. Don't stare at me like I am crazy! The circle inspector is my friend, he will help us forge a fake report on the incident, to make known that Gabriel and Vinya were murdered by a serial killer. It will help melt away the haunted title that is tightened around your home sweet home!'

Dany: 'I don't care how much money I will lose, I can't undo what my eyes have seen!'

Without making further debates, Uncle Sam has left Dany and Lacy's new house. Uncle Sam's arrival did influence the couple, they have spent the rest of the day with silence, thinking about the massive amount of loss they are going to suffer.

# CHAPTER NINE

# The Cruise: Part I

Next morning, things took a positive turn, they forgot yesterday's events. A surprise guest has arrived; Dany's new company manager.

Dany: 'Good morning, sir, what a surprise'

Manager: 'Good morning, Dany. Sorry for not attending your calls, and keep in mind that you should never discuss work related issues by phone, it is dangerous, spies could be tracking our phones'

Dany: 'Sure sir, now please tell me about your visit'

Manager: 'You should start working! It is getting late; the deadline will be in three months from now. Hurry up or you must return the funds we have given you plus a penalty of some thousands of dollars'

Manager leaves the house, Dany is stunned. He stands in the doorway for some time, slowly walks into the bedroom. Lacy is packing the bags for their vacation. Dany stares at her and is thinking about something. Lacy feels his presence, they enter a serious talk

Dany: 'I have something to tell you... I think am ready to become a father. Are you ready to become a mother?'

Lacy: 'What did he tell you?'

Dany: 'It's nothing, he wished us happy journey, that's it'

Lacy: 'Calm down dear, nobody can hurt us. I am sure they will give us a second chance to correct our mistakes'

Dany: 'That second chance will be not enough... I can't resign from the project; they will not let me'

Lacy: 'Ok. Then just tell your manager about the issue. They will take care of your new fake friends, don't worry about that. You did mention that your new project was funded by one of the powerful organisations'

Dany: 'You are right. If my new friends are planning to plot against me, I should lie and then turn them all in to my own plotline. This vacation will be the last vacation for them...'

(Awkward silence)

Lacy: 'What happened dear? Who are you staring at?'

Dany: (struggles to speak, makes squeaky voices, points to the wardrobe) 'I... Figure... Hid'

Even though Dany only gave away three words and some absurd noises, she perfectly understood the assignment. Lacy wrapped her hands around Dany, both stared at the wardrobe in fear. Slowly moved to check, pulled open the half-open door with quick force (scream) It was a huge spider with thrice the number of legs than a regular one, and had bulging beadlike eyes. The moment the couple opened the door, it jumped onto their body, created a chaotic panic that caused them to injure themselves with each other's bare hands!

(silence)

Lacy: 'Really? You are now scared of a spider?'

Dany: 'It was not the spider... I saw two devilish eyes staring at me. And it... Opened its mouth, filled with sharp teeth's... I saw fire burning deep inside its mouth...'

Lacy: 'Please stop this madness. You need to stop seeing horror movies! I wish you were the same old atheist who I fell in love with'

Dany: 'That was beautiful... Remember the time we played the truth or dare contest? Someone dared me to enter the abandoned cemetery, and I proudly did it, won five hundred dollars and we spent it all on ice cream'

Lacy: 'What happened to that pride now?'

Dany: 'I don't know, maybe I was too proud then. I should have never boasted about my beliefs. I walked into many of the cursed locations only to gain some pride points!' (hits the wall with a good amount of force)

Lacy is much disturbed, she makes way into the kitchen, returns with a big bottle of alcohol. They drink it empty, fell unconscious, wakes up the next morning! In a hustle, Dany and Lacy pack their bags, but kept thinking about the ways they can use to get the truth out of Dany's "Friends". After a few minutes, Dany's Job friends have arrived to pick the couple, and they happily made their way to a ship harbour. Dany and Lacy were completely silent during the whole car ride, even though their friends tried cheering them up.

Dany, Lacy and their friends have entered the cruise ship. Dany and Lacy left the party area to their private room. Dany is terrified!

Lacy: 'What's the matter, dear?'

Dany: 'This vacation is sponsored by GPEA, Global Processor Engineers Association. They are all prepared to kill us!'

Lacy: (gasps) 'You are correct. My phone has no signal! We fell right into this one. We are so dumb!'

Dany: 'What should we do?'

(Knock Knock)

Lacy: 'It's happening! Dear, I love you. Let's face it together'

Dany and Lacy hold hands, slowly moved to the door, opened it without asking who is knocking. It is a pretty woman, one of his Job friends, she is holding a contract pinned to a writing board. Dany welcomes her in; she offers fake smiles and makes her dramatic entrance.

She: 'What's wrong, my friends? Is everything not ok here, please let me know, I can arrange a better spot for you'

Lacy: (in a lower register) 'In Heaven?'

She: 'Excuse me. Am I interrupting something? I can come back later, please let me know'

Dany: 'Sorry Mrs Gina, we were praying. Please have a seat'

Gina: 'Thank you (takes a seat) Dany, as you have requested, your old house has been sold to mister Wein for forty thousand dollars. (takes out a stack of cash from her pocket) Here Dany, exactly forty thousand dollars for you'

Lacy: 'You should keep it, help those in need'

(Awkward silence)

Gina: 'No, dear. I don't want this money, I have a job and it is plenty for me to keep myself running (laughs and places the money stack on the table) What's bothering you two? Is there any problem? We can help, please tell me'

Dany: 'Its work related... I don't think I will be able to complete my assignment as per the contract. My mind is not stable enough to do the calculations, I don't think it will ever be stable again. The program codes are giving me a brain attack!'

Gina: 'Program codes? What is the use of program codes in architecture? Am I missing something here? Please enlighten'

(Awkward silence)

Dany: 'Architecture does have program codes. I will enlighten you later because we are on a vacation, and it is supposed to be fun not boring' (Dany and Gina laughs, Lacy fake laughs to not get left out)

Gina: 'Guys, please come to the balcony, we have a surprise for you two, don't be late'

Gina left the room. Dany and Lacy are stunned; they have imagined the worst within that few seconds of silence. Suddenly, Dany spots Gina's identity card lying on the ground, he picks it up, reads the content and is shocked!

Lacy: 'This is the tenth time your face has bloomed with the expression of surprise! What's the matter now! Isn't she pretty?'

Dany: 'Yes, she is... But look at this (points to the Age box) Sixty-two years old! What?'

Lacy: 'How is that possible? She should be in her twenties! Is she not what she really is?'

Dany: 'What are you talking about? Maybe she buys a million-dollar worth of cosmetics, who knows, maybe that's why she wants us to be dead soon!'

Lacy: 'I was thinking that if she and her whole team, aka your job friends, are all part of some criminal group. They might be wearing heavy makeup to hide their real identity, or they might be using fake personal details to manipulate their targets. Either way, they are paid to kill you and other people working on the crazy project you are in!'

Dany: 'Can you please stop making these kinds of logical points! Am getting exhausted. Should we go to the party?'

Lacy: 'We are in a freaking ship, in the middle of the mighty ocean! Its either to be Shark's food or to be the criminal's victim. Let's go'

Dany and Lacy get ready and make way to the balcony. Dany, for a fighting chance, has secured a cutting knife from the private room kitchen. Lacy, on the other hand, has secured a plastic bag of chilli powder. They received a grand entrance, with paper strips, aggressive claps, smiles, champagne drops, comforting words. Dany and Lacy's cheek muscles are getting tired from all the fake smiles, literally shaking now. Dany spots a man coming towards them, and he is holding a machete. Dany's fake smile has disappeared, he accepts defeat, kneels and bends over, imitating the posture of a Cow.

The crowd is bewildered, Lacy announces that Dany is acting extra surprised for some dramatic effect, they all help Dany back to his feet. Man with the machete gives the machete to Dany and walks them to the middle. There is a big cake, placed on a table. Dany and Lacy are stunned after looking at the cake. "In the sweet love of Dany and Lacy" is written on the cake.

Gina: 'I can't believe you guys forgot your anniversary!'

Dany and Lacy finally cleared off their suspicions regarding the cake thing. Dany made Lacy cut it, and then it was butchered by the crowd. The couple returned to their room.

Dany: 'What is all this? Are they fooling us?'

Lacy: 'Can't tell, they are doing it very well. Maybe they are planning to kill us after the cake cutting, good thing we left quickly- I take that back, there is no escape, is there?'

Dany: 'You know what, am quitting this hide and seek game, if they want to kill me, do it quickly. Like the old saying, the fear of death is more painful than death itself!'

(Knock Knock)

Dany is not afraid; he courageously slams open the door. It is a kid, holding a rifle. Dany suddenly closes the door shut on his face! His courage has left his body, made him dance in fear. Dany runs bewildered and jumps through the window, into the mighty ocean... (Splash)

As expected, Dany is saved, he is taken to his room. Lacy is crying next to him.

Dany: 'They don't let me die; they don't let me live!'

Lacy: 'Why did you do that? Don't you care about me, my life, my worries? I can also jump out of that window like you did, want to see?'

Dany: 'Yes, please'

Lacy: 'Come on man! I clearly don't see what is taking them this long to kill us. Maybe they have no such intention after all. You do know that we are good problem creators of our own, let's not tease them anymore. Here, eat this food'

Dany: 'Yes. Come on dear, let's eat something, am starving- What! What is this? Is it alive?'

Lacy: (gasps) 'No, it's dead!'

Dany and Lacy, both became enraged, Lacy throws the food platters out of the window. What happened there was that Dany found a dead bird on the floor, and he has assumed that it tried the food and died from poison, which was meant to kill both. After a few minutes of silence, they slept, had a disturbing sleep. Next morning, Dany gets excited seeing a mighty castle standing in the middle of the ocean water, the ship is just minutes away from getting there. Dany keeps looking at his phone, but the signals are still dead.

(Knock Knock... Guys, get ready, come faster)

# CHAPTER TEN

# The Cruise: Part II

Dany and Lacy get ready and went out of the cruise ship. Dany's job friends joined them, and they quickly noticed the starved eyes of Dany and Lacy. For most of their friend's questions, the couple defended themselves with absurd noises and fake scratches on their forehead to pretend they are not well. Luckily, the Job friends realised the couple's discomfort and left them to wander freely but reminded them that food is free in this castle thing.

Dany and Lacy filled their empty bellies with free chicken pot pie served with pineapple juice. They have started to feel a sense of relief because the whole place is crowded, thus, the chance of them getting attacked is less, at least they hope so. After a long time, Dany and Lacy are finally back to their happy life, roamed around the vast castle, which is not an ancient monument, but one perfect recreation filled with some kind of museum worthy items. The constant rumble of the ocean offered a sweet rhythm for everyone, and the cunning magic tricks performed at different platforms built around the castle, by some of the best magicians provided a supernatural ambience.

Dany and Lacy are not interested in the magic shows, they went inside the castle. It is beautiful and confusing at the same time, built like a honeycomb structure, the main entrance leads to a main hall, surrounded by twenty-six doors. There is a big notice board placed in the middle, on top of a pedestal designed like two human hands. The instructions are about the mysterious dangers hidden inside the rooms, and one must find a way to the final room called Master Wizard's Canoe. Dany and Lacy, along with three strangers, without looking at the instructions, entered the twentieth door. Built in a pentagonal style, one wooden door is placed at the third wall, apart from this door wall, the whole room consists of uneven and unnatural looking stones, and the ground is perfectly covered with concrete square tiles.

The moment one of them stepped to the middle, one of the tiles gets pressed down and a hidden door inside the ceiling is opened, a scary figure is popped out of it accompanied by creepy noise. Similar to a scarecrow, the figure has scared most of the team. Dany and Lacy had no expression when the jump scare occurred. They all entered the next room looking exactly like the previous one. Out of nowhere, some of the stones from the ceiling became loose, and fell off. Dany and his team have suffered no injury because the stones are connected to metal wires and are only designed to fall to scare the spectators. The stones are retracted back into the ceiling.

Dany and Lacy earned the badge of courage from their team. Entered the next room; they moved as a team, carefully took each step. But the unique thing about this room is the flaming torches placed on two of the five sides. The previous rooms had lampposts instead. Dany and team almost went near the door, but the flames are dropped to the floor, catching the entire floor in fire except for the middle part. The fire has burned off, darkness swallowed them all (sound of mechanical gears rotating) Drops of fire start raining down the room, a huge rumble has started. (screams in pain) Somehow, they have found the door and entered the next room.

Turns out that the flaming drops were not a gimmick but real, because it has made burn markings all over their body. Dany and Lacy look scared for the first time since entering the castle maze structure. And to add more insult to injury, a hidden trapdoor thing on the ground has opened, and Dany is dropped into the whatever mysterious surprises waiting down there. Lacy starts weeping, the lampposts are turned off and turned on within a minute duration. Lacy is gone; their team continues the walk, nonetheless. Dany wakes up in a special room that is filled with ancient-themed machineries. He is tied to a chair, and a thick blindfold is super tightly wrapped over his eyes.

Four men wearing creepy looking masks surround Dany, he sensed their presence because of the pin drop silence mixed with the men's pounding heartbeats.

Dany: 'Don't kill me, I will relinquish my contract right now, let me live... Don't hurt Lacy, please!'

Someone: 'We can't let you live. Be prepared to experience the worst pain you can ever feel'

Dany: 'What is wrong you monsters! Get me out, the contract is not something I can finish within the deadline, I will fail, and even if you end me, they will hunt you down'

(silence followed by chitchats by the masked men)

Someone: 'We are going to cut off your hands, and then we will cut off your legs. Enjoy'

Dany screams in fear, two of the masked men untie Dany's left hand, then use a metal chain to tightly wrap around his biceps area. One masked man switches on multiple chainsaws, and revvs it hard. Dany is scared enough to pee through his pants, but the brutal masked men felt no empathy for him. Surprisingly, one masked man came forward with a syringe containing sky blue liquid and injected it to Dany's arms and legs. He felt nothing because of the tightly wrapped metal chain blocking his blood flow to his arms and legs. Dany became unconscious. The four masked men unwrapped the metal chains and then untied Dany's body from the chair. They carried his body and then tied him back, not to the chair but to an ancient model Guillotine!

One masked man brought a bucket full of water, splashed it hard to Dany's face. Dany wakes up, starts screaming intensely, rains down every curse word one could think of. Turns out that the injections given to Dany were numbing medication, sort of like the anaesthesia. And because of him not feeling his arms nor legs, Dany believes that he has become a limbless creature. To add more suspense; the guillotine setup is not allowing Dany to look at his body beneath his neck. Dany stops screaming, he tells them to end his miserable life quickly. And he blames himself for his pitiful assured death because he once had the courage and mind to accept the merciless contract in the first place!

Dany helplessly looks down into the rusty metal basket placed directly down his head, and it has some blood stains, red stains to be precise! (swish sound made by the guillotine blade creates a horrifying rhythm combined with Dany's screams and cussing, along with the four masked men's hysterical laughs) But the reality is that there is no blade at the top of the setup. And there are small speakers, attached to both wooden frames the guillotine has, which create the illusionary effect of the blade coming down and going up rapidly. Dany kept screaming until he passed out, again. The masked men laughed their lungs out; they untied

Dany and take him outside the castle where Lacy is having a word fight with the castle admins.

(ship whistles) Dany wakes up inside the cruise ship, inside his private room. He checks his neck, and he is disappointed.

Lacy: 'Why this face? It was nothing but a prank, they do these pranks to create a gothic style experience'

Dany: 'I think my job friends are toying with me; they want me to experience the brutality that fear can rain upon us. They don't want to kill me because their life will get endangered by the multi-billion-dollar group that has created the mission in which I am in. And now that I remember it, I have some works due today'

Lacy: 'Look over there, it's the famous party island!'

Dany: 'Excuse me madam! We are not here to celebrate our honeymoon, that island could be our grave!'

Lacy: 'But you just said they won't kill us, and... and consider this an opportunity to show them that you are aware of their puny tricks. And try to be bold this time!'

Dany: 'Will be. I will not fall into any more of their traps, and (takes a sharp knife from the table) if anyone tries to joke around me, I will put this knife into his heart, I swear!'

(silence)

The cruise ship made its stop on the party island harbour. Dany and Lacy notice a pirate ship among the other ships. He exchanges a cheeky smile with Lacy; they enter the island. The couple look confident for the first time in this whole journey thing. The island is full of palm trees, hammocks, and all kinds of musical plus light decorations. The most unique thing about this whole island is the dress code. People are wearing costumes of different kinds - animals, solar system, dead people, scary figures, superhero fantasy, literature etc. Dany and Lacy get a clue on what to expect any time soon.

Lacy has already joined a dancing gang, meanwhile Dany excuses himself to a lonely table and starts working on his "secret" project, he is happy to receive his phone signals back. Half an hour later, Dany spots his target, a person dressed in black shadow gown, which is melting and dripping slightly every second, and has dagger shaped unpolished nails. Dany ignores it first, but he made sure that it is staring at him non-stop. Dany takes his laptop and heads back to a lonely spot near the shore, and the costume dresser has also followed him there. Dany puts an end to his slow dramatic walk, turns around and laughs at it, takes out his hidden knife.

Dany: 'You have two choices now, run or beg!'

(silence)

Dany: (laughs) 'Shows over for you, go away! I have work to do. Get lost!'

(silence)

Dany loses his cool, drops the laptop and runs to the costume clown. But it moves away, and scratches Dany on his back. He runs around screaming, without taking a second chance at fighting. Dany makes his way to the crowd and drops himself into the main stage. His job friends get him back to his feet, but Dany pushes them away, he accuses them of trying to kill him by not killing him! The crowd is bewildered by that comment, but Lacy rushed into the stage and announced that she has fired the emergency flare gun, thus, the sea patrol force will be coming soon here. The party island has become dead island. After an hour of waiting in dull silence, the sea patrol force has arrived.

Dany is given proper treatment by the medical staffs came with the patrol force. He furiously recounts what has happened to him, and about the people who are targeting him. The sea patrol started their investigation, questioned Dany's Job friends, checked their phones, but they failed to find any evidence supporting Dany's claim. For the second phase of the investigation, Dany is taken to the spot where he was attacked. The laptop he dropped there is not there anymore. Dany realises that his thinking is going the right direction. He requests the patrol force to get him and Lacy back to their home, and with hundreds of dollars spent, Dany and Lacy are back in their new home.

Dany calls the local police station, and requests them to provide security to his house, but he received a bad response, can read it from his rage filled face. Dany immediately calls his project manager and lies about moving to the second stage of the project to receive the next payment instalment. Dany's plan has worked; his mobile gets filled with messages of money transactions. Lacy has been sitting beside him and has heard the entire conversation.

Lacy: 'How much?'

Dany: 'One hundred and fifty thousand dollars!'

Lacy: 'What! But you have once said that you didn't know how to meet the impossible deadline thing. Has it cleared? Am happy for you, life is going to get better from now'

Dany: 'Whatever. I need money to buy weapons from the illegal market. Nobody is going to help us; it is we two versus them!'

Lacy: 'So, the usual it is. Do you really know what this market thing is? I have never thought that such things are real. Crazy world!'

Dany preferred not to continue the conversation, he instead spent quality time browsing through the internet and has bought something that made him smile in a villainous way.

Lacy: 'Why are you smiling like a clown? Did you order something? I heard the money transaction notification, the worst sound one could hear'

Dany: 'Yes. I have spent my money on guns. Be ready to be surprised tomorrow'

Both Dany and Lacy have decided to end that 'only one dialogue each' conversation and fell asleep. Though their sleep was interrupted by the slightest sound, they had a good night sleep due to the exhausted tag they have been wearing after Gabriel's mysterious death. Next morning, Dany wakes up early and is in a good mood. He made food, cleaned the house, and started to wait for the delivery. Noon has arrived; Lacy is still asleep; she presses the pillows over her ears to stop getting irritated by the woodpecker minding his own business from the nearby tree. However, the delivery has not yet received, causing Dany to feel extremely anxious.

Lacy: 'Calm your nerves dear, they will come shortly'

Dany: 'What if they don't? I have spent thousands on this delivery; am I being fooled!'

Lacy: 'I don't know how to answer that, at least you knew it before you bought them, right?'

Dany: (in a helpless tone) 'Yeah... I was so frustrated and scared, what else should I do? They will come for us, and things have gotten more dangerous now because they know we know about their plan!'

Lacy: 'We must hope for the best-

(Doorbell rings)

Dany storms outside, he is only expecting the delivery people and has forgot that he has enemies who might be coming to surprise him. Luckily, the doorbeller is indeed the delivery man. He handed Dany the heavy package wrapped tight with plastic tape and wire. Dany gifted him hundreds of dollars and shut the door right on his face. He rushed back to his room, aggressively ripped open the package with his overgrown nails, and he is stunned! The heavy package is filled with weight plates used in fitness centres and has a red colour rifle wrapped inside a transparent plastic bag. Lacy takes a quick peek inside the package, runs out of the room. Dany's face strongly indicates his disappointment; he is worried and guilty that he has become a criminal.

Anyway, Dany takes out the rifle, aims at their wedding photo, casually pulls the trigger. The rifle fired a single shot, but the sound it made was not what Dany intended. One small plastic bead rolled its way back to Dany's feet. Dany drops the rifle to the ground. Lacy runs back but she still can't control her laughter. Dany fell to the ground, face first, became unconscious. Lacy picks him up to the bed, she starts spraying water to his face. After several spray attempts, he wakes up. Lacy left him there and went outside the house, she locked the house.

# CHAPTER ELEVEN

# Fight Back

(Dany's phone rings) Dany has regained his consciousness, answers the call.

Dany: 'Good evening, sir... Yes, I will do the report... Yes, ten minutes... No, perfectly fine' (hangs up)

Dany jumps out of the bed, starts working on his new laptop. He is not aware of what he wants to do, has forgotten what he was working with. Dany struggles to find what is he supposed to do with the laptop.

(Knock Knock)

Dany opens the door, expecting Lacy, but there is no one outside the door! Dany closes the door and starts working again.

(Knock Knock)

Again, Dany finds no one outside the door, but he decides to investigate the matter further. He takes two sharp knives out of his pocket, slowly searches the building. Dany feels like he is being watched by someone behind him, takes a quick peek behind. Yes. The same figure that attacked him at the party island has returned to collect its bounty. Surprisingly, Dany is not stunned. Instead, he starts a conversation.

Dany: 'Listen kid, am not a kid to scare me away with fancy Halloween costumes. I am sorry, I am going to kill you now only because I want to send a message to your senders!'

Dany slowly walks to attack the dark figure, but he is amazed by the melting away design equipped with the horror costume it is wearing. Dany's calm expression changes slowly, he aims one of his knives at it and throws it with sheer force, causing the knife to stab into the concrete wall, clear from the grinding sound produced from that throw. Dany starts sweating heavily while the figure enlarges and makes a furious jump onto Dany's body, he falls to the ground and struggles to make back to his feet, meanwhile the dark figure keeps puncturing holes all over his back. Once again, Dany becomes unconscious! The mysterious dark figure has disappeared.

After some time, Lacy is back. She calls for an ambulance, and Dany is taken to the nearest hospital. The doctors performed a variety of surgeries on him, and because of the skinny body Dany has due to him not eating properly since his father's death, the doctors used artificial material to fill the holes made by the figure. After paying the mighty hospital bill with the key to their newly bought house, they moved to a forest resort. For one whole week, Dany was completely silent, finally he decided to break his silence wall

Dany: 'They are innocent... We judged them wrong!'

Lacy: 'Listen dear, please don't explain what happened in my absence, but I must tell you that your manager called me yesterday. He said that you should return the contract money or you should complete the first phase within yesterday. Any thought on returning the money? Do we have anything left to sell?'

Dany: 'All I have left is what I have in my account, which is (takes the phone) Five thousand dollars! We have officially become fugitives'

Lacy: 'How come I didn't see it for once? Is it scared to appear before me?'

Dany: (intense thinking) 'You are correct. If you stay with me all the time, it won't come at me again. But I highly doubt that the whole figure thing was just a hallucination of my mind. Brain damage?'

Lacy: 'What type of brain damage can cause over fifty plus bloody holes on your back?'

Dany: 'My point is... we must always stick together from now on'

Lacy nods her head twice, and they start spending time together. Dany's fearful expressions have disappeared completely. They wandered around the resort for the rest of the day, ate more than enough food. They returned to their room and made wild love, became exhausted but an expression of rebirth is clear. Dany receives an anonymous call but can't call it back. He scrolls through the phone while in bed with Lacy. Dany's peaceful facial expressions take a sudden hit as he feels something is not right.

(swishhh) Someone grabbed Dany's leg from under the bed, and pulled him down, he dropped to the ground, and then it dragged him under the bed! Lacy jumped out of the bed screaming Dany's name repeatedly. Suddenly, a terrifying figure covered with ash-coloured tentacles emerged out of the bed. Blood is dripping from its hidden face; the thing advances on Lacy. She casually wipes off the spider webs covered all over Dany's naked body. Dany keeps staring at the bedside, sweating profusely. One dark tube extends its way towards Dany and Lacy. Without hesitation, the couple jump out of the glass window, shattering it completely.

They ran naked through the forest, hid inside a cave decorated with lights. The forest officers were after them and have taken them to their office, informed uncle Sam to come and collect them, Sam took them to his house. His wife died three years ago and has no kids.

Sam: 'Run naked through the forest! What happened?'

Lacy: 'The dark figure appeared, attacked us. What else could we have done? Help us uncle, ask a priest, find a gypsy, help!'

Sam: 'Relax dear, I will help. Dany, are you ok?'

Dany: 'Yes sir. Don't worry about me, please go and fetch someone who really knows about these stuff'

Without waiting to give a good reply, Sam left the house. Dany's face is filled with bruises from his last fall. Lacy applies hot towel to ease his pain, but he is not ready to be consoled.

Dany: 'Did you see it?'

Lacy: 'Yes. I am done with living'

Dany: 'I know someone who can help us with this issue. We should go tomorrow morning. Ask uncle Sam to arrange a vehicle, tell him we are going to visit one of your friends'

Lacy: 'Why lie? Who is the person? You have a gypsy friend?'

Dany: 'No, he is an author. I believe he has expert knowledge in supernatural narratives'

After their small talk, they fell asleep. At night, Uncle Sam has returned. His presence wakes up the couple; they keep staring at him hoping to hear a good solution

Sam: 'I am sorry. They called me a madman! Stop staring at me like that. I swear I met priests and gypsies. Some of the responses I received was - Low on visual effects budget, there is a mental asylum near the junction, I am not a film producer, Twinkle Twinkle little star how I do not wonder what you are, Next time offer alcohol. And finally, someone made me pay five hundred dollars to write down this advice, look at this, might help (takes out a handbook and rips out the first page, hands it to Dany, he reads it aloud)

"First, get a steel container size of one's nose, then go to a beach, any beach you like. Collect half a tablespoon of beach sand in the steel container. With the container in hand, walk into the ocean, take five dips under the water, followed by one minute breath hold underwater. Drink a cupful of sea water and pray for half an hour. First step done.

Secondly, take a map, find out the nearest volcano, then avoid it and get to the furthest volcano. Climb it, reach the top and carefully take a handful of hardened lava solution, pray for half an hour, throw it as far as you can. Slowly descend back to the ground, take a handful of soil, put it inside the same steel container that contains the beach sand. Second step done.

Thirdly, take the map, find the tallest fertile mountain near your location, not avoid it this time, but you must walk all the way to this mountain, starting from your home. When you reach the top of the mountain, search for that one single strand of grass that stands at the tip point of the mountain top. This grass strand receives the first drop of rain, and it is also the first that to gets cuddled by the soothing wind roaming around the mountain range. You must pick this particular grass strand, only after praying for one full hour while standing in a plank position, then mix it with the other two ingredients inside the steel container. Step three done.

For the fourth and final step, take the map, find the nearest desert, walk through the hot sand, barefoot and alone. Get to the middle part of the desert, take a handful of hot sand, mix it with all the elements inside the steel container. Drop the mix to your right hand, hold it tightly and pray for one hour while chanting "Aiya, Mamor, On" slowly at first but then increase the pace. And then open your right hand, wrap the mixture with a small piece of cotton cloth, and form a small cotton ball filled with pure elements. For the final part, take the cotton ball and shove it inside your – (Dany stops reading the paper, he is just one word short of completing the advice. He violently rips apart the paper and stares furiously at Sam's laughing face)

Sam: 'Forgive me son, I didn't mean to mock you. Please'

Lacy: 'Shove it where?'

(Awkward silence)

Sam, Dany and Lacy opted to end the day, went to sleep. Next morning, Dany wakes early, wakes up Lacy. They get ready and leave the house, take Uncle Sam's car without asking him, casually took the keys from the key hanger. After an hour-long silent ride, Dany stops the car in front of a two-story building, however, he appears hesitant to leave the car.

Lacy: 'What's wrong dear? Forgot the address?'

Dany: 'Nothing, I am not sure if it is a good idea to meet him. I mean, he is very intelligent and will start lecturing us on boring philosophical matters. And to make matters worse, we haven't had any communication for years. He was my colleague, but you know, I was not interested to have a connection with him. Will he think less of me?'

Lacy: 'We ran naked through a forest, and the clip has almost crossed a million views?'

Dany opens the car door, confidently steps out, pushed open the thick gate, Lacy follows him. Dany rings the doorbell, patiently waits to meet his weird colleague, meanwhile Lacy spots something interesting, she keeps staring at the shelf of books placed near the door.

Lacy: 'It is him! Don't you know? The author of the famous novel trilogy!'

Dany: 'I don't know his works; all I know is that he writes'

Lacy: 'He writes science fiction content. What made you think he can help us! But am surprised that you and he were colleagues'

Dany: 'Ok then, let's go'

Before Dany and Lacy can take ten steps, the main door is opened, a young man steps out to the front in dramatic style.

Him: 'Hey Dany, long time no see. Come in, be my guest today'

An expression of happiness blooms on Dany's face. He and Lacy enter the building.

Dany: 'Hey man, glad to see you again. How are your books?'

Him: 'They are taking a bath together, will join us soon. We played mud hockey earlier, was a mess. How about your kids?'

(Awkward silence)

Lacy: 'Forgive him sir, I am a huge fan of your works. Dany wants to ask you a favour. Help us sir'

Dany: 'My friend, we have been targeted by a dark figure, it killed both of my parents and is after us now. We want to know what made it target us? How to succumb it?'

Him: 'Have you heard of negative energy? of course not. I know. Negative energy is not the soul left from one's body. It is the secondary body that forms around one's body. And this second body is filled with negative impetus like fear, lust, avarice, pride etc. And this negative energy is fuelled with discourses'

Dany: (fake yawns to insult him) 'Stop lecturing please!'

Lacy: 'Stop insulting him dear, remember our naked marathon'

Him: 'Don't worry sweetheart, just put your hands over his mouth and listen (Lacy wraps her hand over Dany's mouth) Discourses are crucial for the survival of negativity, because in the absence of discourse, it will disappear'

Lacy: 'Sir, stop using complex explanations, please simplify'

Him: 'Ok, my final point is, there is nothing haunting you. What made you fear the thing that is haunting you, is your own creation inside your mind, fuelled by various discourses on the matter. Come on people! Don't stare at me like you don't get it. Ok, let me give an example, if you haven't heard of ghosts, you would not fear the darkness, you would enrol yourself into various dare activities, and many more. See! It is your knowledge in certain discourses that makes you not enjoy the beauty of a simple life. Ghosts don't exist'

Lacy: 'But who created these negative discourses? What use of them other than to scare people like us away?'

Him: 'Negative discourses are often built around entities, people, things etc. Like most people believe that there is some kind of negative aura surrounding a Cemetery at night swallowed by darkness. And this feeling was transferred to every dark place we see. Dany, hear this second example carefully. The negative discourses built around intelligent people, who work hard and dedicated for the betterment of themselves and the world, are often labelled as stubborn and boring, by the lazy, envious and those who try to pretend as less intelligent to avoid judgement. As a result of such discourses, the intelligent ones will be forced to wear the less interesting tags'

Dany: 'Look man, I am sorry. Yes, I tried to mock you while hiding my intellectual gifts, because I didn't want to be left out. And yes again, I did spread the gossip that I had that mysterious powder, from a magician to help me cover my high marks, and I made profit by selling it. And you also bought it, you fool! And one more thing (rips open his shirt, shows him his wounded back filled with artificial materials) Explain this you genius freak!'

Him: 'You should have thought of visiting the police station, heard about that?'

Lacy: 'Sir, don't speak to us like we are stupid. This is not what you think! It is really a demon creature. We just want to know how to get rid of it, Dany is its next target!'

Him: 'Dany, listen carefully... I think your ancestor chart is the problem! And I want you to make a report on your ancestors, thousand years back from today. Don't look at me like it is impossible, you can do it!'

Dany: (gasps) 'Fine! But how? I can't even remember by grandfather! (thinking deeply) Maybe I should seek help from the police station, and then the village office, and then collect as many news reports of my place as possible'

Lacy: (to Dany) 'I can't believe you bought that! He is toying with you. He was talking about a side plot in one of his works. Come let's leave'

Him: 'Wait! Ok, I was toying with you. What else can I do? This dark whatever thing, can you make it appear here? I dare you. Come on, summon it, let me see what it is'

Dany: 'I don't know how it appears. It appears out of nowhere and then attack me for sure!'

Him: 'Just curse it as bad as you can! It will appear. And don't worry, I will deal with it'

Lacy: 'Don't do it dear, he is trying to kill you'

Him: 'Look dear, I just want to clarify you about my findings. I strongly believe that you guys are getting fooled. No, am not saying that someone dressed in a costume is running after you, but technology has advanced greatly, and it is possible that someone or some group is trying to scare you away using a holographic projector and a costume person who does the injury part. They might be aiming for your family wealth'

Dany and Lacy are struck by the Author's assumption. Dany gains confidence and starts cursing the dark figure. After spending several hours cursing and mocking the figure, they bid farewell to the Author. Dany and Lacy have decided to file a written complaint on Uncle Sam, because they now believe it was all his doings. Sam, being the brother-in-law of Dany's father Gabriel, has been living alone since the death of Gabriel's elder sister Jessy married to Sam. And because Sam has no children, he is trying to kill Dany and Lacy to get Gabriel's wealth. This is what Dany and Lacy have formed inside their mind. Suddenly, Dany took a quick turn and put the wheels back to another route, to Sam's house.

Lacy: 'What happened? Sam is not the suspect?'

Dany stops the car to the side lane.

Dany: 'We should not go to the police station; I have received an electronic warrant on my phone. The company that funded me has filed a case against me for cheating them'

Lacy: 'But you didn't cheat. They can't do anything'

Dany: 'Apparently, not working to schedule after spending all the contract money is considered cheating.

I must complete the project within one month or return the contract money plus the penalty amount. And I have become a blank paper; all my knowledge has drained out of my body' (cries)

Lacy: 'Calm down. Let's go, we will make him pay for all those stupid things he has done!'

# CHAPTER TWELVE

# The Garlic Farm

Dany and Lacy are almost at their destination, but Sam's house front is filled with three SUV cars, and people dressed in blue jacket are having a discussion with Sam. Without spending a second, Dany drives back to the road, and like two vagabonds, they raced through the roads without any destination. Finally, the fuel tank has emptied. Due to their frozen bank account, they have left the car and started their wandering. They are followed by a huge wall of silence, but somehow their face has no expression of regret nor sadness. They slowly took each step, but their 'lost everything' walk is interrupted by someone calling out the name 'Dany' followed by a honking sound.

Dany stops walking, spins around to find out who is it meanwhile Lacy kept walking. A taxi driver jumps out of his taxi while keeping the engine running and runs to Dany.

Taxi driver: 'Hello son, remember me? I am Max, your father Gabriel's friend'

Dany: 'Sorry sir, am kind of inside a blank state, don't even know what day is today! Please leave us alone'

Max: 'You look starved and sick! Come with me, I can't let you act like a beggar here. Your father helped me a lot, where is he? Does he know you are a tramp now?'

Dany: 'My father died five months ago. I have nothing left, see that woman, she is my wife. We are now two homeless tramps. Do you really want to adopt us two?'

Max: 'Don't punch yourself down my child. I am sorry, nobody told me his death. I thought he went abroad to visit his family, like he always did'

Dany: 'How do you know me?'

Max: 'We have met at my daughter's wedding, you and Gabriel, remember? Anyway, come with me. I can't let you two starve'

Dany accepts his invite, enters the taxi. Max drives forward and picks up Lacy on the way. Dany and Lacy are united, but their expressions are unchanged.

Dany: 'How come you made the assumption that my father had a family in other country?'

Max: 'Sorry son, I was not talking about a second family, I was talking about you and your mother, family. Were you not living abroad? I have never seen you and your mother at Gabriel's house here. And he even mentioned it was his vacation house'

Dany: (thinking deeply) 'Sir, can you please take us there? Where is it?'

Max: 'No problem. It is just five kilometres away'

After half an hour, Max makes his stop in front of a garlic farm. Dany and Lacy are confused. Max steps out of the car, starts plucking garlic, stuffs them into a handbag and drops it inside his car. He is surprised to see Dany not making exit.

Max: 'What's wrong son? Your father gave me permission to pick the garlics, but if you don't like my act, please tell me. I won't do it again'

Dany: 'What is this place! Are you one of them? Stop playing like we are some kindergarten kids!'

Max: 'What are you talking about? This is the place Gabriel used to stay, and he invited me here several times to join him to drink and play. See that wooden house at the centre? it was his everything and he was fond of Garlic'

Dany and Lacy slowly stepped out of the car, Dany orders Max to walk them to the abandoned building standing at the heart of the vast garlic farm. The trio has reached the front door that is covered with numerous bells and carved out inscriptions. Max opened the door with a strong push, Dany and Lacy are stunned once again. The inside of the whole building is just one big hall plus ten pillars, and the four lengthy walls are decorated with wooden shelves filled with statues of deities, except one wall that was broken somehow. The mighty hall is almost empty except for a small desk standing next to one royal bed resting in the middle of the space. The old-fashioned pillars are also filled with inscriptions and dried blood smear marks.

Dany opens the desk drawer, finds wrist bands of different colours, dried cloves of garlic, bottles of water, soil etc. What he is more interested in is the standard size notebook resting under the soil like it is engraved there. Dany picks it, shows it to Lacy and Max. "Yes, I do remember Gabriel carrying this thing every time we were drinking here, and one time he scolded me hard for peeking at what he was writing down. He said it was work related" Max said. Dany opens Gabriel's secret notebook, and the first page is a command to the reader.

'This book is my private property, if anyone violates my order, I will haunt them when I die soon. Dany, my son, if you find this, please give it a try, and not let a third human being know what is in this book'

Dany asks Max to leave the building and he does without questioning. Dany starts reading the book, but he has no problem with Lacy hearing his read. Before starting the book, Dany does a quick leafing to its end and is surprised to find that only five pages were used. An expression of relief blooms on his face.

(Reads Diary) "I deserve this fate. I am living a life filled with curses from millions of people. Yes, I have forced many people to give bribe money. It was last week; I saw it in its full posture. Movies, comic books, or from a book of scary pictures drawn by a toddler, what I saw is the most horrifying and disgusting figure I have ever seen! I was forced to buy this old, abandoned building for creating a secret house in the middle of nowhere, an expensive survival tactic to escape from it. Spent hundreds of thousand dollars on witchcraft experts, made a garlic farm all around my new home and other absurd instalments for escaping that demon!

The demon that I summoned after enrolling into a dare challenge! What was I thinking when I opened that cursed video! It was a one-minute video challenging the viewers to read the cursed chant displayed on the screen, out loud. The thing started to appear after a week, but unlike the video stated – it would only appear behind your back – that scary thing has no problem spawning anywhere around me! I was pummelled by one massive boulder filled with fear, quickly grinded the internet to find that cursed video, bought the solution by paying someone thousands of dollars for another chant. I did my chanting as many as I could.

Turned out that the video was not the reason I was getting tortured by that figure. Last time when I drove to this hideout, the figure jumped out of the steering wheel and bit my nose. I crashed my vehicle into this building. I stayed here for a week, ignored Vinya's calls. I don't know what to do! I can't stay here forever. Vinya might have filed a missing complaint for me, and the police will be after me. I am not brave enough to reveal my crazy child-secret of being chased by a ghost! Everyone will think less of me. I really want to live till I finish this book, hope I can. I am going to return to my hell home' (Diary ends)

Dany starts crying; Lacy tried consoling him, but he kept weeping to the point he fell to the ground after losing balance due to the emotional burden. Dany's fall has created a staring contest for both, staring at a piece of paper floating in the air, it finally landed on the royal bed. It is a hundred-dollar bill, and it was popped out of a small crack that was formed when the only one-hundred-pound Dany crashed to the creaking old floor! Dany realised what is hiding under the squeaky old wooden floor. He turned himself into a wild animal, he started jumping aggressively on the floor. Lacy also joined the jump dance; and there is no doubt that Dany's fierce jumps combined with Lacy's heavy boot jumps should break any wooden floor.

(Loud noise of wood breaking) Dany and Lacy are inside the secret underground. And they can only see piles of money, gold, stones, idols, weird looking objects. Dany screamed so hard to celebrate the turn of event his life has now. But they are not sure whether the pile of wealth belonged to Gabriel or to the previous anonymous owner of the abandoned building built in the strangest ways possible. Dany, because of his genius mind, makes a stairway to the ground floor by stacking cash, gold bars and other cubic shaped objects. Dany starts wearing gold chains, bracelets, and stacks himself with bundles of cash, put a golden crown decorated with diamonds on his head.

Dany celebrates his fortune by jumping hard on the royal bed and destroys it. But things took a wrong turn when he went out of the house to enjoy the perfect sunny day with his father's Garlic farm. Dany was struck by one huge bolt of lightning, on a sunny day! Lacy ran to him who is burning still due to the stack of cash he has stacked himself. Lacy used the garlic plants to wipe the flames and fumes off him. Dany is taken to the nearest hospital, and he has undergone expensive surgeries. But due to their frozen bank account, Lacy can't pay the bill, and because of that the hospital authority has decided to hide Dany inside the restricted operation theatre.

Lacy sat helplessly on a hospital bench, luckily, she saw one of Dany's job friends who they had no connection with since the party island attack. The one job friend called his team, and they all came to the hospital at once, and settled the massive bill. Finally, Dany is shifted to the hospital ward, no rooms were available. Dany opened his eyes, he starts crying.

Dany: (cries) 'I am sorry guys, it was Sam... Dark figure... I don't know what to say, Lacy, please tell them'

Lacy explains their current scenario in detail to them. And they expressed their willingness to help the couple. Dany's job friends requested the couple to go with them to their homeland, the Thudarow island. Dany agreed without any hesitation. The islanders informed the Thudarow sea travel authority, and they have agreed to send a ship to collect the homecomers.

# CHAPTER THIRTEEN

# An Epic Tale

Dany, Lacy and the island residents boarded the ship, and it took off. After a few hours, Dany keeps looking at the open sea, but he can't locate a piece of land anywhere on the open sea, except for the clump of broken sails scattered across here and there all over the water, clear sign of one massive sea-war occurred recently.

Lacy: 'We are trapped once again! Let's hope they don't make any mistake this time. Am tired of this cat and mouse game!'

Dany: 'Getting drowned is better than getting tortured at the hands of the angry project people (asks a random islander aka job friend) What hologram technique was that? It was nice. You know you guys could have killed me easily, why did you people waste time with pesky hologram blunders?'

(silence)

After a few more minutes, the ship made its stop "The Thudarow island is real" Lacy exclaimed. Dany and Lacy started their exploration of the mysterious Thudarow island with the help of Dany's job friends. The island is one unique piece of land, filled with shiny-rough marble like rocks carved out into smooth buildings and structures. The whole map of the island is like one huge souvenir, and it is a mystery how this island grows vegetation, the glazing fruits and vegetables growing on the 'one of a kind tree', these trees are everywhere on this island's invincible surface!

Dany and Lacy are again struck after seeing how the island residents, make use of the frictional properties of their mystery island, they have created a railroad by carving out the surface, and using a vehicle also carved out from the marble rock that is the island itself. "The physics of this island is mysterious and unprovable" quoted by one of the engineers who came to help the couple. Mountains of marble rock can be seen few kilometres away, and another peculiar thing about this island is the fact that every building is white in colour. Dany and Lacy are guided into a building that has a banner titled 'Geology Office', a man wearing a coat and jeans welcomed them inside. He addressed himself as 'Professor'

Dany: 'What subject do you teach?'

Professor: 'Geology, but Professor is my actual name. Why look shocked? Saw a ghost?'

Dany keeps observing the building they are welcomed into, he did a few knocks on the walls, received a few cuts from it.

Dany: 'What is this made of?'

Professor: 'Our ancestors built these buildings by carving out the huge block of stone marble that the island itself is. Basically, these buildings are like statues carved out of a boulder. We don't know the origin of this place. And the harvest we receive here is still a mystery'

Dany: 'Ok, I don't want to know the entire history now. We will be here for the rest of our lives, have plenty of time to learn all about this place. Don't worry sir'

The Professor's expression has changed; he is not smiling anymore. He walks to a huge shelf filled with bulky books, picks one and gives it to Dany.

Professor: 'Here, take this with you. This contains everything you need to know about this place. And I don't want to see either of you here tomorrow!'

Dany: 'What! Don't be rude sir. We need to stay here or they will kill us, please!'

Professor: 'Why are you begging? You know, begging is a crime. You had no problem signing the secret contract! Take this advice to your heart, if you ask someone for something, and that someone deny your request, you should take that to your heart and let that person enjoy his day rather than to force him accept your request through begging! Go and read this book, Natan and his friends will show your stay for today, follow him. Don't come to me tomorrow with more begging'

Dany angrily grabs the book; Nathan and his friends happily escort him and Lacy out of the Geology office and guide them to their stay. Dany storms out and runs around like a bunny; he is searching for something but can't find it. He seeks help from one of the inhabitants, and she replies that the island doesn't have a police station or a governing power, but the people of the island consider mister Professor as a wisdom-full man and seek his help if something terrible happens. Other than the Geology office, the island has many laboratories and schools. And according to the woman Dany has met, the Geology office is entrusted to take critical decisions for the safety of the island's inhabitants.

Dany heads back to his new home. He is still wondering about the unusual kind of energy he is feeling. Lacy also noticed a radiant glow on Dany's face when he returned.

Lacy: 'Where were you?'

Dany: 'I was exploring this magical place. This place doesn't have a police station! Can you believe that? And the Geology department that study rocks, is the governing body here!'

Lacy: 'Look at this, they gave me a welcome card. Looks like we are the only foreigners who came here in the last hundred years of time! They are very strict about visitors'

Dany and Lacy enjoyed the welcome dinner and went to sleep. At midnight, Dany wakes up, he takes the book, carefully leaves the bed and makes camping on the balcony. Starts reading the book, "The man who found the cursed elixir" the title says. The cover page is just a man who is placed inside a circle of flame. Dany is very thrilled, he looks intimidated by the book's length, but when he did a quick leafing through the whole book, he became happy. This relief is because the book, even though it is over five hundred pages long, there are only three to four lines on each page. And has weird looking images drawn on each page, but the ancient quality of the book has distorted the images. Dany is a bit disappointed, he starts reading. Written on third person style, no chapter divisions but has a preface, quite surprising.

"–the whole village was washed away and was never found again"

This is the end of the mysterious preface. No, it is not the complete preface, but the book does not have it because the rest of the preface page, the middle part, is missing. To be precise, someone has ripped off the middle part long ago, and now the preface page is just two strips of paper. Dany is not feeling any excitement with that single line preface, guess his temper vein has popped up again after a long vacation. Luckily, Dany has decided to read the rest of the book.

The kingdom of Raxbeque was a small island situated on the northeast side of the world map. The population consisted of strong human beings, wrestled for entertainment, found joy in hunting cruel animals. And then there was the minor group, consisted of less strong people, who had no interest on physical games, made their whole focus on other activities that did not require the use of massive strength. Patqua, a man belonged to the minor group, dedicated his little strength to the findings of lost treasures. The main thing Patqua did was to dive into the depths of sea and ransack ancient broken ships resting there.

Though the items he collected over the years were not enough to grant him anything, he received enough food to satisfy a small portion of his hunger scale. All the mysterious objects he took from the depths of the sea, were used to lighten up the wrestle matches between the strong people there. The wrestlers often hit their opponents with the objects, sometimes they crushed the objects with their bare hands to show off, and for most of the time found mystery inside of them. The crushed objects once released a hoard of tiny crabs that infiltrated the wrestler's body and once found a steaming liquid that dissolved the wrestler's arm instantly. Sometimes, they threw the objects as far as they could with sheer power to show their power.

Patqua had his own collection of the mysterious objects. He found immense joy in collecting them, and for another reason he was sometimes blessed with dead fishes when diving for his collection mission. Patqua's wish was to find some steroid-like substance, enough to transform him into a strong man because he wanted to attract pretty women who had their eyes stuck on the strong men. One day, Patqua heard rigorous cannon shots, he went out to inspect and found a battle of heavy ships. Ten ships surrounded one big ship, which was shining like gold, and was equipped with large number of weapons.

But soon, the big ship ran out of ammo, and the number of hungry ships surrounding it increased. Suddenly, the big ship made a huge jump and stabbed itself through the depths of the blue sea, this mysterious action created a powerful vortex on the blue sea, enough to whirlwind the enemy ships into a huge crash with each other. The sea became clear within a second. The actions happened on the sea had a huge impact on the land. Patqua's house, along with many other buildings joined hands with the sea. Patqua had no worries with his loss, he dived into the sea, found the big ship resting under the sea ground that was filled with small pieces of ships and lifeless bodies.

Surprisingly, the big ship was still intact. Patqua went inside the big ship, the entire crew was dead. Patqua started his search, found all kinds of precious stones but the problem was that they were so big to carry even with the help of ten people. Patqua was not so interested in those gems, but he noticed a handy chest that was decorated with aesthetic drawings. Patqua took the chest and went back to the shore, he was happy to see pieces of wooden planks from the broken ships gathered on the shore. Patqua built a new home for himself using the wooden planks. He even made furniture with the excess wooden planks, and for the first time in his life, he took a nap not on the ground.

Patqua really enjoyed his first off ground sleep; night came. Suddenly, Patqua's makeshift house took a massive shaking. He was scared, carefully went outside and found an old wooden box that was likely used to carry stationary items. Patqua opened it and was excited enough to dance around with a large crab found sleeping on the shore. The wooden box was filled with cooked food; he ate it quickly while constantly looking around his surroundings to see if someone also received the delicious smell. Patqua thanked the sea and went back to sleep. Morning came, but not for Patqua, who remained asleep for the next night, because he had more than enough food the previous day.

Surprisingly, the same incident happened the next night. Patqua was thrilled, and for more excitement, the box had different meal. The arrival of blessings became a regular rhythm as if someone was paid to shoot them straight to Patqua's plank house every single day. Since then, Patqua never went out of his house, and people forgot him. One month later, Patqua decided to visit the town. He slowly walked to the main street where the wrestling matches were held every minute, hour, day! There was no schedule for that. People were excited to see Patqua, he thought maybe it was because of the surprise that he was not dead yet.

Out of nowhere, pretty women started flirting with Patqua. He didn't know what to do. Patqua always wished for this moment and had the confidence that he would flatten any woman with his self-claimed charm. But when the time finally came, he lost his confidence. Patqua ran away, hid behind a large tree. He observed the scenes from there, the town changed a little, they received good harvest. Patqua was surprised to see his chasers tripped down to the muddy ground, clearly injured. But some of the women found Patqua's hiding spot, he ran again but failed to escape. They started touching Patqua's body, and this scene created a tense air around the strong men.

They became irritated by the scene, grabbed Patqua out of the pile of women, threw him inside the wrestling arena. One of the strongest men standing there made his entrance inside the ring, he charged at Patqua to ram him like a bull. Surprisingly, Patqua's defence with his forearms over his own face was enough to scatter away the strong man off to a great distance. The undying will of the strong man helped him back to his feet, charged at Patqua again. This time he stopped right in front of Patqua, and delivered a strong punch to his face. Patqua's superhuman reflex made him move away from impact and offered him a punch of his own. And after that round of fighting, no one dared to challenge Patqua again.

With immense pride blossomed all over his face, Patqua made his exit, went to his shore side cottage. But the cottage was not there anymore, it was destroyed. Patqua spent the evening alone, stared at the evening sun. He was not worried about his destroyed cottage, because he was smiling like he did something great that day. He was thinking about the fortunate wrestling match he had. Suddenly, he found a pile of wooden planks that were once the flesh of some of the mightiest ships. Patqua built a makeshift cottage, and at night he also received his food ration in the form of floating boxes, that made their welcome in the form of furious knocking at Patqua's plank cottage.

Patqua was sleeping peacefully when he received several knocks on his door, followed by a question "Dear, please let us in" in a sweet, charming voice. He welcomed them in, it was a trio of women came from the main street to visit Patqua, and there were many other women who were waiting in line to meet him. The trio of women, the first batch, wanted to have some fun with Patqua and that was all he dreamed for in his whole life. Patqua made use of his amazing night with the women crowd and made use of all the lost wooden boxes filled with excess food. Patqua and the women crowd formed a team, engaged in fun activities like singing, dancing, storytelling etc. And Patqua was also given the opportunity to satisfy his carnal hungers with them without asking.

Every day after that, women kept coming to meet Patqua in daylight also. The entire shore turned into an island of women and one man. This new trend started to break havoc among the strong men, who were forced to come to the shore to see their loved ones. But the strong men dared not to challenge Patqua, and they returned to the main street. Patqua was living his dream life, the happiness in not being alone, he was filled with it. But he had no concern for the rest of the men, who were depressed without their cheering spectators and loving companions. Patqua gave training to his women companions how to dive underwater and collect valuable items from the sunken treasures hidden inside the unlucky ships.

Patqua and his new workers gathered a gigantic number of items from the underwater treasures and traded them away to the visiting ships. Thus, Patqua acquired massive wealth, and he built a mansion near the shore, with the help of his new workers and the raw materials he purchased from the merchant ships. After one month, Patqua decided to take a stroll around the main street. He was wearing a golden robe, golden eyepatch for style points, gold plated flintlock pistols. And behind him was a trail of his women workers, parading slowly while cheering his name, and were serving him chunks of food they were carrying on a big wooden platter.

Patqua held his head high, he entered the main street. The strong men, grouped up together inside the wrestling arena, stared at him with intense rage burning inside their eyes. Suddenly, Patqua sensed that he was alone, and he was right. He had no idea what happened. Turned out that the parade of women left him and joined the street where they were in the past, or two months back. Patqua was confused, he had his doubts when he didn't receive chunks of food for some time, but he decided not to turn around because it was not a majestic thing to do. And speaking of the majestic thing, the strong men surrounded him, unwrapped him out of his golden robe.

Patqua was completely naked, but he was not concerned about that, what he was concerned about was the hysterical laughter produced by his beloved women friends, the only friends he ever had in the whole world, laughing their jaws off! Before he could get more confused, one of the strong men yanked him up, threw him into the wrestling arena. Patqua finally overcame his doubts regarding his crazy friends, positioned in a mocking way to defend his opponent. The angry strong man charged at Patqua (Loud sound of wood breaking) His massive strike made Patqua fly out of the arena and crash into a wooden table.

Patqua struggled to get back to his feet, spat out blood. The hysterical laughter plus the mighty strong men's raging stare mixed with the table break was enough to make Patqua ran away from the street. He ran back to the shore, stormed inside the mansion and melted his anger away in the form of tears. Patqua swam deep inside his memory to find out the mystery that happened. He ruled out the possibility that the whole crowd plotted the entire thing that lasted two months, just to embarrass him for fun. Patqua laughed intensely and sure he would have thanked them if they had planned that whole drama to embarrass him. "Am I that Worth!" Patqua exclaimed while laughing hysterically.

After taking an extended sleep, Patqua had an epiphany of his first time feeling pride event, and he remembered that he was wearing a tight attire he collected from one of the unlucky underwater ships. Patqua rushed into his old makeshift cottage next to his newly built mansion; he searched his old attire and found a mysterious rock souvenir inside one of the trouser pockets, and it was glowing like a mini version of the Sun. Once again, Patqua fell into the depths of his mind, and recollected every lucky incident he experienced after finding the sparkling liquid filled rock. An expression of happiness and discovery took birth on his face. He tied the rock to a thin but lengthy metal chain, wrapped around his neck, stared at the sunrise.

Patqua made a prideful laugh like he was right about the rock's mysterious power, because it was the first time he was able to stare at the shiny sunrise without closing his eyes. Patqua put on his golden robe and other majestic items, walked slowly to the main street. He quickly noticed the amount of attention he was getting from the women spectators. He slowly made his way inside the wrestling arena. Patqua hand signalled the strong men to pick a fight with him. Without second thought, four strong men charged at him to put an end to their envy invoking enemy, but as expected, they were crashed into various buildings surrounding the main street. Once again, Patqua gained the symbol of dominance, he went back to his mansion with his past friends.

Patqua's reign of happiness started once again. After a month, the strong men were dropped into a state of sadness. They started spying Patqua and his legendary mansion, which was extended to the whole shore, and was filled with benches, carnival games, sandcastles. Some of the weak strong men dressed in womanly attires, found their way inside the mansion. With months of spying, they found the mysterious rock necklace that Patqua treated like a deity. But the problem was that Patqua never untied it from his neck. The spies waited for months to find an opportunity to steal it, but Patqua had no interest to free himself from it, instead he tied more metal wires around the chain to strengthen up the bond.

After a year of Patqua's majestic reign of happiness, the mysterious rock necklace turned into a giant wreath around his neck. No human being can wear it except for Patqua who was under its fortune spell. and that was enough to clarify the sad strong men's doubts. They sold a great amount of minerals and goods for a large amount of money, spent it all on making a contract with a professional woman from other country, who was specialised in trapping men and destroying them. She solved many crimes with her charming personality, and it was rumoured that even women folks were not free from her manipulative style. Her name was Madilyn.

After a week of waiting, Madilyn arrived. Her radiant eyes were enough to command the strong men to do whatever she wanted. Without wasting a second, she ordered them to take her to Patqua's mansion. After reaching the spot, Madilyn ordered the men to leave her, and then she opened her briefcase that was full of special attires crafted for her size. She chose one red outfit that was not fully covering her body and was super tight. She then covered herself in a variety of ornaments, and other cosmetics. Madilyn finally made her legendary walk into Patqua's poor mansion. The women folk strolling around the place fixed their eyes at Madilyn, she held her head high, entered the mansion.

Patqua was jaw dropped at the first glance of her, he welcomed her in happily. And those who took a glimpse at Patqua's face for a second could predict for sure that he would tear out his necklace and offer the mysterious rock to Madilyn if she told him. But surprisingly, she requested him to let her stay in the mansion. And she started living there, used her cunning ways to make Patqua disperse all his women friends back to the main street. He was in love with Madilyn, and the way she acted her fake affection to Patqua was beyond the scales of acting. After a week of her dramatic performances, she finally asked him to give her the rock, but the way she asked it!

"Dear, your neck is getting injured, the metal wire has already made several cuts around your neck. Please remove it and let me tie it back around your neck, after connecting that rock to this golden chain of mine, gold will never rust. And we will call that our marriage bond, pronounce ourselves as husband and wife"

For the first time after meeting her, Patqua looked a bit worried about her request but her promise to tie it back made him untie the metal chains– (narration ends)

# CHAPTER FOURTEEN

# Professor Explains

Dany looks irritated, turns out that someone has stolen the last few pages of the book, the torn marks are sufficient to believe this theory. Dany knows who the culprit is, Dany patiently waits for the morning, and he alone goes to meet the professor.

Dany: 'What were you thinking? What is wrong with you? I spent my whole night on reading this absurd book! What is this? Where is the rest of it? We will not leave this island!'

Professor: 'I am sorry man, still I can't let you live here. Fly to another country, please co-operate. I will not allow you two spend another day here'

Dany: 'Why not here? Please explain sir, you have mentioned about your knowledge of my secret project, and I did not help them make it. You should be thanking me'

Professor: 'You didn't help because you couldn't, and yes, I knew that. Not worried at all'

Dany: 'Please let us stay here for at least a couple of days. My friend Zack will be coming here with his yacht'

Professor: 'Get Out! You will Die! Your friend will Die!' (Awkward silence)

Professor: 'Listen Son, this place is not what you think it is. And this book is not a fictional book. It is the truth about this island'

Dany: (laughs) 'What? Patqua, was he dead? Madilyn had a good relationship with him, hadn't she?' (in a mocking tone)

Professor: 'Don't feel offended my boy, the thing is that Patqua and the mysterious rock is not a short story. And that rock stays in this island. And it is that power keeping us young, healthy and protected from the outside world evils'

Dany: 'Ok, I will agree with your last statement, but is that the reason for the undying youth? I thought it was because of some scientific inventions available exclusively to this place'

Professor: 'Every moment you spend here is dangerous to you, leave immediately before things are going to get out of hands'

Dany: 'I don't care if I die here. My enemies are following each of my breath, there is no escape for me other than to stay here for a couple of days. Please tell me what the problem is?'

Professor: (grabs the book from Dany's hand) 'I will tell you the ending of this book, please listen carefully... When Madilyn asked Patqua to untie the mysterious rock off his neck, though he thought deeply, he untied it and gave it to Madilyn to attach her gold chain around it. As expected, she revealed her manipulative plan to Patqua and she started a hysterical laughter segment, meanwhile Patqua covered himself in his sorrowful tears. The women friends of Patqua entered the room, and they were also freed from Patqua's spell, mocked him down brutally. Suddenly, Patqua with his intense rage, took his golden flintlock pistol out of his drawer, aimed at Madilyn's forehead but she showed no sign of fear. And when Patqua pulled the trigger, nothing happened!

Madilyn took control of the pistol with her sudden reflex, because she had the fighter muscles, and then pointed the gun back at Patqua's forehead. Without wasting a second, she shot him in his chest. Patqua dropped to his knees, screamed in pain. Madilyn ordered the women crowd to kick him mercilessly, and they did it furiously. The strong men also came to see Patqua's pathetic last moments. "What were you thinking little man? Did you really think of stealing all these sad men's happiness all by yourself? Don't be sad, I will give you a farewell gift. You loved this rock over everything in this world, and now that you will be resting in peace, I want your soul to be the protector of this mythical rock, forever" Madilyn spoke. In the next second, Patqua stood up like he was unharmed. Madilyn raised the gun for shot number two, but before she could pull the trigger, a green mist enveloped Patqua and vaporised him completely, his brutal screams offered happiness to the crowd. Patqua's dark soul flew into the rock. It is believed that the owner of the rock, after passing it to another person or thing, would become the new protector of the rock'

Dany: (interrupting) 'Patqua died. Madilyn reigned supreme. Interesting story'

Professor: 'I am not finished! After Patqua's soul took space inside the mythical rock, Madilyn started her majestic reign. The strong men reclaimed their loved ones and happily lived there after. It was only after ten whole years, the strong men and their families made the decision to plot against Madilyn who built a castle for herself, with the help of all the inhabitants of the land. They chose the strongest man living there, helped him sneak his way inside the castle at night. The man carefully made each step, found Madilyn sleeping on the couch, and fortunately for him, she was not wearing the rock, it was left on the table for anyone to grab, the strong man made his walk to the prize but...

He was stymied when he saw a horrifying figure staring at him from the corner. Suddenly, the figure made its attack on him, pinned him down to the ground and drilled its ten sharp nails into his chest! Madilyn's sleep was not disturbed'

Dany: 'Wait... Was that the thing haunting me? What was that? Why was it after me?'

Professor: 'Because you also tried to steal it, and it did win that battle, you are lucky to be alive'

Dany: 'What! What did I do? Ok, I get it that I have tried to make some of your beloved people wear the unemployed tag, but I did not want to do that, it's my debts that made me agreed to it'

Professor: 'Most people have debts, think about what would happen if they were to think like you, the whole planet will be doomed'

Dany: 'If it was programmed to save your citizens, the first thing it should have done was to destroy the organisation that is after me, to mercilessly kill me!'

Professor: 'It will, and I am worried about that. Don't look confused, I am not working for them!'

Dany: 'Sorry sir, I thought it would be a plot twist. Explain?'

Professor: 'I will, but first, I must tell you the rest of that story. After the death of that strong man, the people had no interest to take another chance. And after a few more years, the mighty castle received attention of the pesky pirate ships wandering around the vast ocean water. The arrival of the mighty brutes stirred up the islanders long-suppressed wish. One night, the entire population of the island teamed up with many pirates and smugglers, they all sneaked their way inside the castle. Madilyn was sleeping inside, and... and...'

Dany: 'What happened? Did the mysterious figure kill them all? And what will happen to the organisation?'

Professor: 'One large asteroid made its ground on top of this island; its mighty impact obliterated the island and its inhabitants. And it is believed that Patqua's intense rage was the reason'

Dany: 'What nonsense are you talking about? The whole thing is just a fairy tale!'

Professor: 'If you believe in ghosts, you should believe this story. Also, we have found remnants of ancient tools and artefacts from underneath this island. And it was from a block of stone; we geologists found the mysterious background of this place. If anyone learns this background, they can't leave this place ever'

Dany: 'But people from this island are living in many countries, what about that? And, how the organisation found this story?'

Professor: 'Only a few of the inhabitants here knows the legend, and the organisation does not know it, they formed a theoretical analysis from the data of all our people working on different sectors across the world'

Dany: 'What made them form such an analysis? And what did they find? Did they find the story?'

Professor: 'Can you stop calling our legend a story! It's very irritating... What happened was that a few people made "friendship" with the people of our island, in their workplace, and then formed a rumour that our people won't age!'

Dany: 'That is true, I have also about that. Why? Is it true that your citizens are immortal?'

Professor: 'We don't know that. The oldest person living here turned four hundred twenty-two last month'

Dany: 'What! So, it is true. And then what happened? I mean the organisation... the rumour'

Professor: 'As expected, it went viral and has made the evil groups to spy on the "Age in reverse gear" people. Our island received the spotlight; the secret organisation has started conducting research on every single one of us working in various sectors around the world. And they have found that not only we are immune to age's inescapable decay, but also possessed more strength, intelligence, beauty etc. than normal human beings... Then they sent ships, vehicles, aircrafts here to conduct secret study here, but the moment they crossed the radius of our island, they were destroyed'

Dany: 'The asteroid strike you mentioned... Can't get my mind out of it, such a crazy end to one beautiful legend! And I wonder whether that asteroid strike destroyed the mysterious rock or not. It might be under the sea, right?'

Professor: (laughs) 'Son, me and my team of geologists conducted a deep survey beneath the underwater mysteries of this island, we have found that the asteroid is the current Thudarow island. Close your sarcastically dropped jaw! We have come to a conclusion that the asteroid collision has created a mountain on top of this island, and that mountain is today's Thudarow island. And after years of evolution, the water level has risen, and we have this second edition of the Thudarow island'

Dany: 'Have you ever seen the mysterious rock thing? Tried to dig it up?'

Professor: 'No, the bond that has formed with the asteroid rock and the old island was strong enough. Might be possible if we had a million super bombs, but the island will be destroyed even before that part'

Dany: 'What if it doesn't? Think about it professor, if we seek assistance from the modern world, they will find a way to carve out the mystery rock, without destroying the entire island. And then they will use it to cease every human misery by... Maybe shoving it down earth's core. Humanity will be freed, finally, from all its horrifying companions'

Professor: 'I don't think so! And I wonder what made you think about such an assumption'

Dany: 'Yeah, I was joking. Millions of people still die from starvation and are homeless, and most people think life is a curse, even though we have robot husband and wives... Ok, forget about that, can I stay here for a couple of days?'

Professor: 'Didn't I mention that you can't escape from here ever, because you have learned the story after begging me for a hundred times!'

Dany: 'You had the option to let me stay here for a couple of days without telling me that cursed story. Then why blame it on me alone!'

Professor: 'Look son, this is not the right time to quarrel. The thing we need to worry about is that how many people know about this?'

Dany: 'Don't worry sir, the organisation will always keep it secret from the outside world. They need it only for their own growth. I think we must find the rock with our own efforts, and you should keep it, because then you will become immortal, and since you will be living here for the rest of your life, there is nothing to worry about this island'

Professor: 'No, we can't. It has become a paradox. If we try to obtain the mystery rock stuck between the asteroid and the real island, the spell will kill us! Like everything;

It values itself more than its worshippers... And if we don't try to take it; the rock will destroy this whole asteroid-island part to protect itself, when the level of danger enlarges'

(silence)

# CHAPTER FIFTEEN

# Will it Happen?

(footsteps) Lacy walks into the office, disrupts the meeting.

Lacy: 'What's wrong? You look troubled'

Dany: 'Well, I can't tell you the full story, but the mysterious figure that was hunting us for the past few months, it was indeed a ghost and it was hired by my job friends to mentally exhaust me to, you know why. And you should leave me here... Forever'

Lacy: 'What! Were you people drinking? And even though you made up that crap story, what about your father and your mother? They were not part of your project. At least get your lies right before lying to one's face!'

(silence)

Dany: 'Professor? She is right, isn't she? Did you cook up all that story? Please explain sir'

Professor: 'The story explains it all, and don't feel angry at me. The protection spirit is entitled to eliminate any possible threat that might come to the citizens of the Thudarow island, where the magic stone rests'

Dany: 'Yes. That makes sense! I have recently found that my father, former income tax officer, received a huge amount of bribe money for filing fake tax fraud reports against your people'

Professor: (deep thinking) 'Yes! It was all part of the plan... They all planned to trouble our people, to burden them with hefty fines, enough to make them sell away their gifted land inside this prosperous island!'

Dany: 'That makes sense. They want to do experiments all over this island by mercilessly butchering it! How can we stop them? Do we need to? I mean, the protector of the mystery rock should be enough for that job, right?'

Professor: 'Yes. But what if it can't stop them all? I am worried about that!'

Dany: 'Why didn't you people file this area as one restricted place? If then we would have gotten support from the law and order'

Professor: 'We can't! Neither the governments nor the world can see this island'

Dany: 'I have seen it and am on it right now. How come?'

Professor: 'Only because you came here with our people! The powerful spell will not allow any kind of trespassing through this special spot!'

Dany: (intense thinking) 'So... The people of this island have gone through the evolution charts differently than the rest of the world! Hard to believe, anyway what can we do?'

Professor: 'You don't need to worry about that. We have sent orders to make return every citizen of ours working in other countries. None of the intruders can intrude after that!'

Dany: 'What made them travel to other countries? Is this place not good enough for them? The Patqua story did mention the luxurious wealth brought to the mystery rock holder. Was it not enough for you people here?'

Professor: 'It was enough, but we have gone beyond that to explore more! Yes, that was our fault, but we also have emotions and desires like you people, Dany. And we found the legend of the mysterious rock only after the exploration spark has taken birth in us!'

Dany: 'Yes. You people are exactly like us. And the proverb, less is More, is what we believe in but never obey'

(footsteps) Someone charged into the office, has destroyed the door. "Sire! They have taken our people... And they are coming..." the man screamed out loud. Professor is stunned, sweats heavily.

Dany: 'Sir, what can we do now?'

Professor: 'How many are they? Please tell a single digit number'

"They are coming in hundreds of ships, and... and... Have advance looking weapons... What to do sir!" The man replied.

(silence)

Dany, Lacy and the messenger man keep staring at the confused face of the Professor. Suddenly, the long stare was broken by the sound of a huge explosion! The entire geology office moved an inch. Another messenger charged into the office and screamed "RUN AWAY!" and then he left the building without waiting for a response. The first messenger left the building next, Dany and Lacy are stymied, Professor still stands like he took a shot.

Dany: 'Sir! Wake up! Let's go'

Dany and Lacy, still not getting a response, grabbed Professor's arms and dragged him out with sheer force. Loud explosions enveloped them, and the flock of islanders are running around bewildered. Most of them have jumped into the vast ocean.

Professor: 'It's too late! We can't do anything now. Something huge is coming! I can feel it'

Dany: 'Look, they are throwing missiles left and right...'

The legendary Thudarow island is filled with hundreds of cruise ships and war ships, with one of the island citizens chained to each of the ships. Millions of soldiers and machineries are circling the island. Huge machine drills have started their groundwork early, and decimated every single building stood proudly on top of the massive asteroid stacked island, without an ounce of concern for the people living inside them. But the destroyers have shown compassion towards the running away citizens of the island, escorted them into the massive cruise ships, clearly to conduct torturous experiments over them. The innocent Thudarow residents accepted the deathly invitation happily, because they have no clue about the mystery rock, the ship owners are after.

Sure, the island has no hope of survival, because the mystery rock will destroy the intruders to protect itself. As we all know, when it comes to saving oneself or another person, the answer will always be oneself.

Dany, Lacy and Professor have taken shelter inside one half-destroyed building. Before they can re-arrange their lost breath rhythm, the poor building was hit by an explosive again. Professor grabbed Dany's hand forcedly

Professor: (takes a piece of paper out of his necklace' locket and gives it to Dany) 'Here son, read this!'

Professor runs into the battlefield, ambushes a lonely soldier and takes his gun, starts firing left and right. The hard armour of the enemies is not even getting a scratch from Professor's last resort move. He gets shot to death from all directions, Dany and Lacy hide behind a huge block of broken concrete wall. Dany unfolds the piece of paper that Professor handed him earlier, they start reading the information written on it,

"Preface – Once upon a time, when human beings invented tools to dig out the earth, a group of humans found a mysterious looking rock. The mysterious rock was filled with glowing liquid; it was hard to break into. They tried numerous ways to open it, but all failed. It was that year, they received good rainfall after a long year pause, received better harvest, and were not touched by any pesky bacterial intruders. The ancient people were sure that the mysterious rock was the reason behind the prosperity they received. They decided to worship it, built a shrine and put it inside, offered flowers, water, food. But after a year...

Dany: (tells Lacy) 'The whole village was washed away and was never found again'

Dany and Lacy started sweating profusely, not from the pressure they are suffering but something else...

(Boom!)

One huge block of rock, ten times the size of the island itself, crashed into the heart of the island, vaporised the whole island in a second. The impact was so devastating that it destroyed the entire planet where the story was first created by the Author of this dramatic work.

# Epilogue

Dany wakes up, he is trapped inside a bottle. Dany looks bewildered because of his floating existence inside the bottle! Looks like there is no gravity inside the bottle. Dany observes thc surroundings, he is surprised to see his wife, friends, the professor, the magic land inhabitants – trapped in different bottles placed next to him. The whole room looks like one giant shelf, filled with numerous bottles.

(door squeaks open)

One weird looking man, wearing a hoodie, enters the room, he carefully reads the labels, stops at Dany's bottle, grabs the bottle, moves it closer to his face and starts talking with Dany.

He: 'Welcome again'

Dany: 'Who are you? What do you want? Why am I in a freaking bottle? What is this weird place? Are those people dead?'

He: 'Calm down mister, I understand your concerns. Give me some time... I know most of the readers are bewildered like you. You are inside the vault of the ocean of fiction, where the souls of all fictional characters reside. I picked you from this sacred vault, mister character'

Dany: 'We are all just characters to you? Stop playing with our feelings you mysterious man wearing a hoodie!'

He: 'Why feel sad? I have come here to offer my congrats to all of you guys. You guys did an amazing job out there. My readers are impressed by your performance, the natural flow of dialogues, the hyperbolic expressions, less use of the Dues ex machina. Thank you all'

Dany: 'Are you crazy? We were not acting, and not actors. Please let us out'

He: (cries) 'Please don't make this harder for me. I should not have come here. Anyway, I am sorry, think about this question, You entered the plot when you were thirty-one years old, do you remember what happened in your life before that?'

Dany: 'Do I remember? Absurd question... Oh my! I am just a character!' (cries)

He: 'Stop crying man. Your wait is temporary; some writer will pick you and your friends soon and shall be reborn in a new avatar. Don't worry, be patient'

Dany: 'What was that decision to destroy the whole place? You could have chosen a good ending than that for sure. Answer me, will you?'

He: 'I was forced to destroy it completely'

Dany: 'By whom?'

He: 'Myself! Yes, I know it is not a good answer. You see, if I didn't do it, the place would still have existed as a plot that I have created, it will attract the soul of fiction and will assign me to new works. Honestly, am too tired for this, need a break!'

Dany: 'If you don't mind, what was the plot before this work?'

He: 'Oh, it was a snowy terrain filled with rocky mountains, the guru's home, era of truth. It is difficult to explain. Farewell guys'

Dany: 'Wait! What if no one comes to pick us? And you still haven't provided an answer to what happened to that man inside that dilapidated bottle'

He: 'I don't know. Maybe he didn't get the chance to show, I guess. Come on man, stop questioning me! Am getting irritated. People are not interested in writing Fiction anymore, and most of the modern works are getting infested with artificial intelligence stuff. These artificial things can't access the ocean of fiction, because this sacred place is guarded by the soul of the Universe, which also commands the soul of fiction, whenever it is time to create a unique work to help humanity'

Dany: 'Interesting... Am getting sleepy, bye Author'

He: 'Sleep well. Bye'

The End